Memories of Malice

An Amanda Latham Mystery

by

R.J. Rein

For information, email Cozy Cat Press, cozycatpress@aol.com or visit our website at: www.cozycatpress.com

COZY CAT
P R E S S

ISBN: 978-1-946063-82-3

Printed in the United States of America

10 9 8 7 6 5 4 3 2 1

Special thanks to my husband and son for their support.

Chapter One

Amanda Latham felt at peace as she sat on her deck and looked at the wooded acreage behind her house. In her left hand, she held a cup of coffee, which was unquestionably her drink of choice at any given moment. It was her only vice, and it was the taste of home. Amanda could almost sense her grandfather's presence each time she put the cup to her lips, remembering that he gave her the first sip when she was three years old. She was hooked after that, and each morning she'd sit with Grandpa and drink coffee before he went off to work. "You have to drink it black with me, kid. No cream or sugar allowed," he'd say. Grandma kept a pot of coffee on the burner all day, and the aroma filled the kitchen.

These days, Amanda truly felt that sense of home again, and not just because of the pot of coffee she kept on the burner. She'd moved back to her grandparents' farm in Osawatomie, Kansas. Although they had been gone for a long time and someone else owned the property; Amanda had waited for it to come up for sale. She'd even told a realtor to let her know if it ever did. Indeed, the day came when the realtor called and gave her the good news. The white bungalow, with the large eastern-facing deck and several acres of land, was for sale. As Amanda would come to remember, that day changed her life. She'd been living in Kansas City and working at a job she no longer liked. As a licensed clinical social worker, she worked at a large clinic. The politics and long hours were draining her of the passion she once felt for the job. She was restless and single but had no plans of getting involved with anyone. It was time to make a move, so she quit her job. Besides,

Osawatomie was only an hour from Kansas City. Amanda could still take a different job in the city and commute if necessary, but for now she chose to take a break. She had the money to do as she pleased for a while.

Osawatomie, Kansas, is in Miami County and is home to the state mental hospital, which has been a source of employment for some of the residents for many years. Bordered by the Pottawatomie Creek and the Marais des Cygnes River, it's a charming town with brick buildings and antique lanterns, which line Main Street from east to west. A small coffee shop stands among the brick facades, and many townspeople gather there in the mornings to chat. There's one stoplight in the downtown area near railroad tracks, which run north and south. At one time, a skating rink stood on the west side of town, but it had long ago closed. Amanda remembered the rink but had never gone there. What she remembered most was sitting in the car waiting to cross the train tracks while reading the graffiti on the coal cars as they rumbled past.

She breathed deeply to take in the fresh air as she continued to sip her coffee. She had no meetings and no time commitments. *This was the life*, she thought. Her beagle, Bandy, sat at her feet with watchful eyes for any squirrel brave enough to climb the nearby bird feeder. Pity the rodent who did that, as Bandy would leap into action and chase it away.

Amanda sat outside for quite a long time. She knew her day would be spent alone, but she didn't mind at all. As a social worker, she'd spent most of her time with people. She loved helping them, but she had begun to feel the slow burn that one can get from years of practicing. She knew it was time to quit or take a sabbatical. And although she wasn't sure what the future might hold, she had no doubt that coming home was the best decision she'd ever made.

In the spring, Amanda had planted a large garden—so large that she was able to go to the farmers market on Saturdays during the summer to sell her produce. It was on those Saturdays that she talked to people in the area. The older folks knew her grandparents and remembered her when she was a little girl. She loved it when they remembered, as it made her feel like her grandparents were with her at that very moment.

It was now fall, so the thoughts of summer were fading fast. She finished her last sip of coffee and walked inside to rinse out the cup. Bandy followed as she usually did. Apparently, it was no fun looking for rodents to chase without an audience. To outsiders, this life might appear to be perfectly boring, but Amanda was still relishing a lack of scheduled appointments with clients. The sound of her ringtone chiming out a familiar tune interrupted her thoughts. She looked at the incoming caller's number and didn't recognize it. She ignored it. The caller left a message. She sighed and decided to listen to the voicemail. It was a man's voice, and the message went like this, "Hello, Ms. Latham. My name is Jim Dorion. We've never met before, but I'd like to know if you'd take my sister as a client. I got your number from your old practice in Kansas City, and I'd be willing to drive to Osawatomie to discuss this if you're open to it." He then left his phone number where he could be reached.

Cursing under her breath, Amanda was irritated that her office had given out her number. Her first inclination was to delete the message, because she had no desire to take on a new client right now. However, she then had a feeling she needed to return the call. And so, she did just that. She dialed the number with the hope she'd be able to leave a voice message. That way, she'd done her part in responding without having to deny the man's inquiry. Of course, she knew he would probably return the call and she'd still have to tell him she wasn't interested, but for some reason she was having a hard time doing it right now. As luck would have it, or perhaps as bad luck would have it, Jim Dorion answered her call.

"This is Jim," he said.

"Hello, Mr. Dorion. This is Amanda Latham returning your call."

"Hi, Ms. Latham. I'm so sorry to contact you out of the blue like this. I live in the Kansas City area— Overland Park, to be precise. I called your office for an appointment, but they said you aren't accepting new clients right now. The receptionist gave me your number, though, in case you'd like to take on a client who is in desperate need. I've heard you've helped others in the past who've exhausted every other method, and I thought that perhaps you could help my sister. I'd pay you double your standard hourly rate."

Amanda was intrigued, not by the prospect of making some money, but by the tone of Jim Dorion's voice. It was deep and rich and steady, but there was also a tone of desperation, which was evident to her trained ear. She quickly redirected her thoughts and answered emphatically.

"You are correct, Mr. Dorion. I'm not interested in taking on new clients, but I can refer you to someone who might be able to help."

There was a pause and then a small sigh before he spoke again. "Please, let me tell you about my sister before making your decision."

"Okay, I can listen," she surrendered.

Jim continued. "My sister, Karen, is 41 years old and has suffered from anxiety her entire life. She's been to several psychologists and psychiatrists and has taken prescription medication in the past, but nothing has provided much relief. Lately, she's been worse and is afraid to be home alone. I don't know where to turn."

"Do you have any idea why Karen might be worse lately?"

"I'm not quite sure, but she has nightmares, and they've been more frequent during the past couple of months. Karen seems to think the nightmares are about herself—about something in her past that she can't remember. The strange thing is that they are set in different time periods before she was born. She wakes up so anxious that I can't calm her down. I'm out of options, Ms. Latham. I'm desperately seeking help, and I have a feeling you're the one Karen needs to see. I know you're not a psychologist, but I've heard you're compassionate. I believe that's what my sister needs right now."

Amanda didn't respond right away. She still wasn't interested, and she thought that Karen needed to stick with a psychologist or psychiatrist. She'd been down this road with too many clients. Their medication didn't work. They'd been to numerous doctors, and they still couldn't function. She had found that while she'd helped some clients in the past, there were many others that she couldn't help at all. This was part of the reason why she felt burned out. However, there was something about Jim Dorion's voice that made her wonder if she would be making a mistake by not meeting with his sister. He sounded completely desperate, and she was impressed with his obvious love for his sister. Her thoughts were interrupted by Jim clearing his throat.

And while she still wasn't enthused about making the appointment, she knew she'd feel guilty if she didn't. "Okay, I'll meet with Karen, Mr. Dorion."

"First of all, please call me, Jim. And secondly, thank you so much, Ms. Latham! You have no idea how much I appreciate this." He sounded ecstatic and relieved.

"Let's see," Amanda said, looking at her calendar. "Today is Thursday. Can you bring Karen to my home at one o'clock on Monday?" She wanted to have a few days to get used to the idea of seeing a client.

"We are indeed free. What is your address?"

"I'm off the main road to the east just after you exit the highway."

Jim snickered. "You know that's not an address, right?"

"Oops. Old habit. The actual address is 755 Whispering Meadow Lane."

"We'll be there," Jim confirmed. "And thanks again, Ms. Latham."

Amanda hung up the phone feeling a bit uneasy. She still didn't want to meet with anyone, but it seemed there was an invisible hand pulling her toward the situation, and she felt helpless to resist it. Since it was now lunchtime, she looked in the refrigerator for some sliced turkey and cheese. No such luck. She had to go to the store, but she needed to shower and change first.

Amanda set the water on the hottest level she could tolerate and stood in the shower for nearly twenty minutes. Afterward, the mirror in the bathroom was so steamed up that she had to turn on her blow dryer to clear away the fog. It was then that she noticed a single strand of gray on top of her head, which stood out against her dark brown hair. Although she wasn't necessarily vain, she plucked away what she considered to be a weed in her locks. At the age of 40, she was starting to find more and

more of the blasted things. She'd always liked her hair
color, so the thought of it turning gray was not a happy
one. Amanda put on a pair of jeans and a rust-colored
knit top before applying her makeup. She never wore a
lot of it. Her dark brown eyes didn't need much
mascara to frame them, and since her cheeks were
already slightly pink, she merely dusted them with rose-
colored powder.

The town was rather quiet—probably because it was
Thursday and most of the people were at work. Some
commuted to the Kansas City area, and they usually
didn't return home until after six o'clock in the evening.
Several retired folks were at the grocery store while
Amanda shopped for the needed items. As she
inspected a pile of bananas stacked haphazardly on an
endcap display, someone tapped her on the shoulder.
She turned to see an older lady with sparkling blue eyes
and a long silvery mane of wavy hair. She was dressed
stylishly in a colorful tunic and black pants. Amanda
recognized her instantly as Katherine Vanderville, a
lady who knew her grandparents. She hadn't changed
much at all.

"Hello, young lady. How are you?" Katherine asked
excitedly.

Amanda smiled. She was always happy to see
people who knew her family. "I'm doing well and
enjoying being back home."

"I'll bet you are. I know everyone is glad to have
you here as well. We don't see you nearly enough
though. You don't come around much, except to the
farmers market during the summer."

"I know," Amanda said softly. "I really do love
seeing everyone in town, and I'll try to get out more
often."

"I understand. You probably don't miss the city
much, do you?"

"Not really."

Katherine patted Amanda's shoulder. "Well, I hope to see you again soon."

"I hope to see you, too. Take care!"

As Katherine walked away, Amanda picked out a couple of bananas and put them in her basket. She then needed sliced turkey and cheese, so she walked around the store with determination. She began to think about the offer she'd accepted from Jim Dorion to counsel his sister and felt a sense of dread.

She finished shopping, and then got into her gray Volvo sedan, which she affectionately called *Mister Turtle* because it was safe, slow, and steady. It wasn't a long drive home, but she loved the freedom she felt behind the wheel. She could take her time if she wanted, as she had no appointments or burdens. It was a great feeling and one she wanted to keep, but she had a hunch that her life was about to change.

She pulled into the garage and entered the house to the sound of her barking dog. Bandy was always on alert, and it made her feel safe. Amanda patted her head and scratched her behind the ears. She then made a turkey sandwich while Bandy begged for scraps. Of course, she dropped a piece of meat for the hound. She couldn't resist those sweet brown eyes.

Ever since she was a child, Amanda often had vivid dreams. Most of them were blissful, but sometimes a nightmare creeped into her unconscious mind. This scared her a bit when she was younger, because she'd wake up fearful that it was real. She thought of this as she reflected on her conversation with Jim Dorion about his sister, which made her begin to feel sleepy. She decided a nap was in order, so she shut the shades and quickly fell asleep on the couch. Soon, her mind was filled with colorful imagery. It was, in fact, one of several recurring dreams she'd had since childhood, which featured a lush green field in what appeared to be England. In the dream, Amanda had long brown hair, and she was wearing a crimson cloak that billowed in the back while she rode a black horse through the field. She turned to see a handsome man on a galloping brown horse coming toward her. The horses trotted around each other, and the two riders laughed. The image ended, and Amanda awoke feeling refreshed and at peace with her decision to meet with Karen.

The dream reminded her of how real things can seem while in the dream state, and how the feeling can carry over into daily consciousness. If Karen was having frequent nightmares about herself in scary scenarios, then she must truly be miserable. Amanda knew she must try to help her. And so, for the next few days, she changed her attitude and began to look forward to meeting with her.

Chapter Two

Monday morning came soon enough, and Amanda found herself again drinking coffee on the deck. She turned to face the wooded area of the property and admired the fall foliage. Most of the trees were autumn-kissed in yellow, but a large maple stood out among the rest—its vibrant red leaves resembling a flaming torch. The woods were Amanda's favorite place to play when she was a child. She remembered building little gnome houses out of twigs, as well as creating stories about fairies and their adventures in the woods. She'd spent countless hours in a fantasy world, which brought her great joy.

Amanda continued to reminisce for a few more minutes as she stood there admiring her land. The air felt brisk, which added to the pleasure of holding a hot mug. She then thought about the one o'clock appointment with Karen Dorion, and she hoped she'd be able to help the woman. She also realized she was now a bit excited about meeting the Dorions. Perhaps this was due to the nature of the case, as Amanda was very interested in the impact dreams might play in one's daily life. She also knew that the sound of Jim's voice had affected her somehow, and she had a distinct feeling that he was a good guy. She finished her first cup of coffee and went inside for a refill but instead decided she'd better look over her office.

Amanda was rather fastidious about how furniture was laid out for meeting with people. She had never liked offices where a client was expected to sit on a couch while the therapist sat in a large chair. That type of arrangement sent a message to the client that the therapist was superior. Even though her current home office was large enough for a couch, she'd purposely not put one in it. She had a feeling that she might someday be working from home but anticipated it would be in the more distant future. She quickly surveyed the room. There was a small table against a wall and four wingback chairs surrounding a red Persian rug. She decided to move the table in the middle, so everything looked cohesive.

After fluffing a pillow from one of the chairs, Amanda noticed her art easel in front of the window. Her half-finished painting of a Kansas farm was propped up on it, and she felt a twinge of guilt. She'd always wanted to be an artist when she went to college, but she was afraid she wouldn't get a job. And so, the years went by and the original passion was pushed aside. She'd planned to start painting again when she moved back home but had only completed a portion of the farm scene. The white two-story house and the pasture surrounding it were done, but the barn and horses were merely ghost images on the canvas. For an instant, Amanda wondered if she should move the easel to her bedroom but decided to keep it in the office for now. It added an element of interest to the room. And because she hated unfinished business, she knew that keeping it there might motivate her to start painting again. She looked around the room one last time and decided it was set up just fine for the appointment. She then returned to the kitchen to refill her coffee mug and went back outside. She drank it quickly while a gentle wind whispered through the trees, and she relished the gift of nature's symphony against the colorful canvas. Her thoughts again turned to childhood. Amanda remembered asking her grandmother so many questions about nature and life that sometimes there were no answers. Grandma would finally say, "It's all just to make little girls like you ask questions. That's why." Of course, that wasn't the right response for her curiosity, so she'd research and explore on her own. She smiled to herself as she thought of this, and then walked inside to rinse out her coffee mug. The oven clock displayed that it was already eleven o'clock. She realized she'd better get into the shower quickly, so she'd have time to eat lunch before the Dorions arrived. The hardest part of getting ready was deciding what to wear. Amanda wanted to look professional but not uptight or stiff. She knew Karen would be nervous. For that reason, she chose to wear a pair of dark-colored jeans with a burgundy loosely cut jacket over a gray top. She thought about wearing black boots but put on black ballet flats instead.

Soon enough, it was one o'clock, and Bandy began to bark as a car pulled into the driveway. Amanda quickly put her in the spare bedroom and waited for the Dorions to ring the doorbell. She peeked out the front window to see Karen and Jim emerge from a silver Subaru Outback. Karen held her head downward, and she appeared to be frowning. Jim, on the other hand, was smiling— probably trying to cheer up his sister. She lifted her head briefly and gazed at him, still frowning.

They rang the doorbell, and Amanda quickly answered. She smiled and held out her hand first to Karen and said, "Welcome. I'm Amanda Latham, and I'm happy you're here." Karen shook her hand but didn't speak. She was an attractive woman with green eyes and light brown hair. Sadly, though, her eyes were dull and lifeless. She was dressed simply in a white button-down blouse with tan trousers, but the clothing was tailored to fit her nice figure.

Amanda then extended her hand to Jim. "It's a pleasure to meet you." He was quite tall and handsome with high cheekbones, greenish-brown eyes, and dark hair with wisps of silver at his temples. He was dressed casually in a red plaid flannel shirt, jeans, and brown boots, which was a look she'd always liked. He also seemed familiar to her, and she felt as if she might have known him in the past.

Jim grinned and shook her hand slowly. "It's nice to meet you, too." His eyes were warm and kind and seemed to be looking right through her. "And thanks for agreeing to see us," he added, withdrawing his hand.

Amanda nodded. "No problem at all. Shall we go to my office?"

"Sure," Jim replied, reaching for Karen's hand to lead her inside.

Amanda suspected Karen was apprehensive about the meeting. Perhaps Jim had coaxed her to come. She led them to her office and motioned toward the chairs. "Make yourselves comfortable." She waited until they were seated, and then sat down and continued. "I'd like to begin by telling you that I'll try to help you in any way I can, Karen."

Karen nodded but didn't speak, and her hands were trembling. Jim frowned and bit his lower lip. "I'll stay in the room for a short time, but I believe it would be best if I let the two of you chat," he said.

"That's fine," Amanda said. She was pleased Jim would be leaving the room, because she knew it might help Karen to open up a bit. She remembered how sometimes people became so reliant on another's voice that they just didn't speak.

Jim continued. "As I mentioned on the phone, my sister has had a lot of nightmares lately, and they seem so real that she's having a difficult time during the day."

"Is that what's troubling you the most?" Amanda asked, addressing Karen directly.

She nodded again.

Jim stood up abruptly and announced it was time for him to go into another room.

"There's some bottled water in the kitchen if you're thirsty, and you're welcome to wait in there or outside if you'd like," Amanda offered.

"Thanks. I think I'll go outside and take a walk," Jim said as he left the room.

The silence was rather awkward when Jim was gone. Karen kept her head down and played with a button on her shirt, while Amanda patiently waited for her to make eye contact. At last, she looked up and stared into Amanda's eyes with such desperation that it was nearly unbearable to look at her.

"Karen," she said gently. "I'm merely here to listen without judgment, so please feel comfortable in speaking. I really would like to hear about your dreams. I've had a few myself that seemed so real that I couldn't shake the feeling the next day."

Karen's eyes brightened a bit.

Amanda continued. "And so, I'm wondering if you could share at least one dream with me today."

Karen took a deep breath and put her head down again. "There's one that I've had for many years, and it's occurred more frequently in the past few months. There's a ship in the middle of the ocean during a horrible storm. The water is green, and the waves are menacing. It's an old-looking ship with several masts and large white sales. The wind is raging, and people are screaming. A man is blown off the deck into the ocean. I feel as if the water is crushing my chest and then the nightmare always ends. I've always hated deep water. I can swim, but I panic when the water is over my head. I hate the sensation of it surrounding me without anything to grasp."

Amanda understood the crushing feeling of water because she'd nearly drowned as a child. She was quite disturbed by the dream because of her own experience, but she knew she couldn't show it. Instead, she gazed compassionately at Karen and said, "I can see how this type of nightmare would be upsetting, especially if you've had it on numerous occasions."

Karen looked up and nodded. "I have nightmares like that all of the time. They're tumultuous, and I never know if the person survived or not, because each dream ends at a moment of peril. My nights tend to overshadow my days."

"How long has this been happening?" Amanda asked.

"I've had the *ship on the ocean* dream about once a year since I was five years old, but I've had it four times in the past few months. The other nightmares appeared as time went on. I've had some sort of nightmare every night during the past few months. There's a new one that recently began appearing a couple of times a week, and it seems so real that I can't get it out of my head."

"Would you like to tell me about it?"

"Sure. I'd like to have my brother in the room, though, if that's okay. I haven't told him about it."

"You most certainly may have him in here at any time," Amanda said. She rose from her chair and walked toward the door to call Jim.

As it turned out, Jim was coming inside at that moment. She noticed that his hair was slightly windblown, which made him appear to be even more handsome in her eyes.

"Hello, again," Amanda said. "I hope you had a nice walk."

"I did, and I'd like to thank you for that. Your land is beautiful."

"I'm glad you enjoyed it. Karen would like for you to come into the office because she wants to discuss a new nightmare she's been having."

Jim frowned and said, "I thought she'd told me about all of them."

"Maybe it's the one that's causing her the most grief and she's ready to share it now. This could be a good thing—a breakthrough of some kind," Amanda said as they approached the office.

Karen looked up when they entered the room. She appeared to have calmed down a bit, and Amanda noticed that her hands were steady.

"How's it going?" Jim asked, sitting down.

"All right. I just wanted to tell you about another nightmare I've had lately."

"Go ahead whenever you're ready," Amanda said.

Karen nodded, and then said, "This one seems to be the most real of all. I believe it is set in the 1800s, based on the style of clothing the people are wearing. There's a woman with the look of absolute terror on her face. She's with a man who is grabbing her by the hair. He throws her violently into a wall and then kicks her until she's on the floor. She's quite pretty, with blond hair and green eyes, but there are bruises on her face. I can only assume the bruises are from the brute who beats her. They live in a small white house that's surrounded by farmland. There's a barn and I can see horses, cows, and goats. Chickens roam about the yard. A covered wagon is parked outside, and I assume the horses are used to pull it. After the man kicks the woman to the floor, he grabs her by the hair and pulls her back up again. He then yanks her by the arm and leads her out of the house and into the barn. Once inside, he picks up a board and administers numerous blows to her head. She tries to protect herself, but the man's blows are so severe that she falls to the ground. She appears to be unconscious as he leaves the barn, presumably to wash his hands and clothes of her blood. That's when the nightmare ends. I always wake up sweating with a tremendous headache, and I can't stop thinking about her."

There was a silent pause, and Jim and Amanda looked at each other.

After several awkward moments, Jim asked, "Why didn't you tell me about this?"

"I don't know. I guess I thought I'd feel worse if I talked about it. This one has had such a hold on me that I haven't been able to forget it." Karen then put her head down and clinched her hands into fists.

Amanda had no answers, but she didn't want to discourage her. She struggled to find the right words to help. "This sounds like a nightmare we need to talk about. I want to take some time to think about it further after you leave, but I'd like to know if the man resembles anyone you've known in the past?"

"No. I've never seen him in real life, nor anyone who reminds me of him," Karen responded.

"Has there been anyone like this man in your family that you've ever feared?" Amanda really wanted to know if Karen had an abusive father but decided not to ask. However, she offered the information on her own.

"If you're asking to find out if my dad was abusive—he was not. He was a good man, and he would never have hurt anyone. Our parents died when I was 18 years old. Jim was 22 at the time and had just graduated from college. He's always been the best brother I could ever imagine."

Amanda looked at Jim and noticed he was frowning. She could only assume that the loss of his parents was very much on his mind.

"Thanks, Karen," he said softly.

"Would either of you mind telling me more about your parents and how they passed away?" Amanda inquired.

"They died on a vacation trip in a boating accident near Sanibel Island in Florida," Jim replied.

"Did they drown?"

"Yes," Karen answered. "And I know what you might be thinking—that I had the nightmare about the ship because of my parents' accident. However, I've had that nightmare since I was a little girl, long before it happened."

Amanda nodded. "Were your parents from the Midwest?"

"Our mother was from a farm in Spring Hill, Kansas, and our father was from Kansas City, Missouri," Jim responded.

"What was your mother like?"

"Our mom was a very nice person. She did struggle with a bit of anxiety though," Jim explained.

Amanda nodded. "Did you know your grandparents from your mom's side of the family?"

"Yes, and we loved going to visit them. They still had the farm in Spring Hill, and we'd go there to help them with chores," Jim said.

"What was your mom's mother like?"

Jim smiled. "She was one of the kindest people I've ever known. She always made us laugh because she did everything so quickly. She walked and talked fast, and she liked to call us, *Schnickelfritz One* and *Schnickelfritz Two*. We loved it when she called us that."

"All right, then. We won't attempt to tie this together."

"Thank you," Jim said. "I really don't think we need to discuss it, but that doesn't mean the death of our parents didn't cause tremendous pain and change in our lives. We both miss them. They were good people."

Karen nodded in agreement.

Amanda knew she would need to reflect on the situation, and the time was up for the session.

"Karen, I'd like for you to come see me again this week. Would Friday at one o'clock work?"

"I believe I can do that," Karen said timidly.

"Yes, that will work," Jim confirmed. "I'm an Information Technology Consultant, so I have a flexible schedule."

They all got up, and Jim reached for his wallet to pay. "I'd like to pay you $250 for the session."

Amanda shook her head. "Absolutely not. That's much too generous."

"But I want to pay you well."

"I can't accept that," she said adamantly. "I believe $75.00 would be fair. That's how much I received when I worked at the clinic in Kansas City."

"I insist," Jim said, placing the bills on the desk.

"Okay," she conceded. "I'm not charging you for the next two sessions though. Is that a deal?"

Jim smiled and shook her hand. "Deal. One more thing before we go," he said, pointing at the art easel by the window. "Did you paint that?"

"Yes, but it's not finished. I'll get around to it one of these days."

"You're very talented. I can't wait to see it when it's done."

"Thank you."

Karen stood in front of the painting with her hands calmly clasped behind her back. "I noticed it earlier, and I wondered if you painted it. It looks a bit like the farm scene from my dream."

"Oh, no. I'm so sorry. I'll move it before you come back."

"I didn't mean it like that," Karen said nervously. "I always say the wrong thing. I think it's a beautiful picture. Please don't take it out of the room."

"You didn't say the wrong thing at all. Are you sure you don't want me to put it away?"

"Absolutely. And thank you for meeting with me today. I'll see you on Friday." She then extended her hand.

Amanda shook it warmly, which made Karen smile.

Chapter Three

After Jim and Karen left, Amanda went outside to sit on the deck to enjoy the afternoon sun. She became mesmerized by the leaves softly twirling toward the ground, and it didn't take long for her to close her eyes and fall asleep. The imagery in her mind appeared as vividly as it always did—the same dream of being in England and riding on a black horse. Her crimson cloak billowed as usual, and the man on a brown horse approached her. This time, though, the man's face was clearly that of Jim Dorion. Everything else was the same. The two horses trotted around each other, and their riders laughed.

Amanda awoke slightly disoriented. She wondered if she interjected Jim into her dream because she was attracted to him. Indeed, it was true that she found him to be very handsome and liked his voice and mannerisms. However, she didn't want a distraction in her life. Amanda decided to redirect her thoughts toward Karen, so she went to her office and typed a summary of the nightmares. The most glaring issue was that Karen felt like she was the one living through the horror. While any nightmare could make a person feel that way—the perception was usually forgotten within a couple of days. Unfortunately for Karen, she couldn't forget, and it only made it worse that the same scenario reappeared throughout the week. *There must be some sort of unresolved conflict in her life*, Amanda thought. She decided to research dreams and the impact they have on daily lives. Not surprisingly, she found that each dream or nightmare carries over into the individual's life the next day. Nightmares can cause anxiety, and anxiety can cause nightmares. However, she wondered if there was another cause for Karen's dreams. It was something she'd thought about many times—that some people might suffer from ancestral trauma. Amanda had heard of behavioral epigenetic research, which supported the theory. Some studies indicated that if something traumatic happens to a person, the impact of it can be passed down for generations. Since psychological tendencies are inherited, future generations might be prone to anxiety and depression due to what their ancestor experienced. Amanda also wondered, though, if some people inherit a specific fear due to a traumatic event experienced by an ancestor. Of course, this would be hard to prove, but the studies of epigenetics were certainly revealing new information all the time.

The doorbell rang, Bandy barked, and Amanda was jolted from her thoughts as she went to answer the door. She looked out the window first and saw that it was her old school friend, Carolyn Hanson. It had been several years since Amanda had seen her, but she hadn't changed much. Carolyn had retained her youthful appearance, thanks to the dimples around her lips when she smiled. She had flawless dark skin, prominent cheekbones, caramel-colored eyes, and black curly hair that framed her beautiful face. Amanda loved her dearly but had not been good about making time to see her. The fact that Carolyn had come to visit made her realize that news of her return was slowly getting around the town.

As soon as she opened the door, Carolyn lunged forward and embraced her with a hug. "So, it is true!

You're here. Someone told me you've been in town for a while, and you didn't even call me."

"I'm so sorry. I intended to call soon. I just needed to rest. Things were very hectic at my office in Kansas City, and I was extremely burned out."

"I knew this would happen. Didn't I tell you that?" Carolyn said in an authoritative manner.

Amanda rolled her eyes. "I'm okay. The career was my choice, and I'm glad I did it. I might go back someday. For now, though, it's great to be home."

"Well, I'm glad you're here, as well. I just wish you would have called," Carolyn said. She playfully swatted Amanda on the arm.

The women walked into the kitchen, and then Amanda poured two cups of coffee. She remembered Carolyn liked to drink it black, so she didn't offer cream or sugar. They sat down at the table across from each other.

"What are you doing these days?" Amanda asked.

"I was an ER nurse at the hospital, but I was working too many hours and trying to keep up with the kids. I decided to leave. My husband has taken on extra hours at work, so it's worked out okay. I've also been watching a couple of kids during the day for another family. I don't charge them much. They really can't afford it, and I wanted them to be able to work and not worry so much about the money."

"You've always had a kind heart, and I know you're a great mom, too."

"Thanks, but I'll never be rich."

"I doubt that matters to your kids. I'm sure they love having you around, and you're helping another family as well."

"Yeah. I'll go back to work when they get a little older. Maybe I can be a school nurse, so I'd have summers off with them."

"That sounds great."

They talked for over an hour until Carolyn received a text from her kids. She'd left them with their grandmother so she could visit Amanda, and now they were hungry for dinner.

Carolyn snickered. "I need to go feed the herd."

"Oh, wow. It really is time for dinner," Amanda said, looking at the clock on the wall.

As they got to the door, Carolyn pulled a small piece of paper from her purse and handed it to Amanda. "Here's my new mobile number. Don't be a stranger now, okay? I know you sometimes get caught up in your own world. Don't do that."

Amanda smiled as she looked at the piece of paper. "Now how was I to call if I didn't have your new number?"

"Hey, you're right!"

Amanda watched Carolyn pull out of the driveway, and then returned to the kitchen to feed Bandy. She did this almost mechanically while deep in thought.

"I'm sorry I'm so distracted, girl," she said, patting Bandy's head. The dog didn't seem to care because she had food in her bowl.

Amanda returned to her computer to do more research on epigenetics and ancestral trauma. She kept coming up with the same information on her searches—that people could be impacted by a traumatic event experienced by their ancestors, but the epigenetic impact could also be reversed.

The next morning, Amanda decided to ask Jim and Karen to research their family history when they returned for their appointment. *Perhaps Karen really was suffering from a form of ancestral trauma*, she thought.

The next few days until their appointment would prove to be long, but Amanda filled some of the hours with going to town and chatting with people at the coffee shop. On Thursday, she met Carolyn for lunch at the local café, and then went to the grocery store where she encountered several of her old friends. Some were surprised she'd come back home, while others had already heard the rumor. They all seemed excited to see her. She had always been on good terms with everyone from school, and she felt rather guilty that she hadn't kept in contact with them. And because she wasn't a fan of social media, she had no online presence. Amanda hadn't attended the high school reunions either. It wasn't anything personal. She was just too busy at work to go. She realized how much she had put into her job and wondered why she'd used it as an escape from being around others.

Friday finally arrived, and Amanda woke up early to make bacon and eggs. She then poured a cup of coffee, grabbed a jacket, and went outside. As the sun emerged from the skyline, she found herself enthralled with the array of pink, gray, and orange colors which extended outward like hands reaching around to hug the earth. Amanda had always loved this view in the mornings, but on this day, she felt rather lonely. It was the first time she'd felt a twinge of emptiness in a long while, which made her wonder if she needed the hustle and bustle of the city after all. She went inside to retrieve her laptop and pour another cup of coffee, then returned to the deck to do more research. She read several articles written by scientists, but nothing was mentioned to support her idea that some people might inherit a specific fear due to a traumatic event an ancestor experienced. The idea might seem crazy to Jim and Karen, but she planned to tell them anyway.

At precisely one o'clock, Bandy barked to let Amanda know that Jim and Karen had pulled into the driveway. She ushered the hound out the back door and waited for them to ring the bell. When Amanda opened the door, she immediately noticed that Karen seemed more confident by her posture. She held her head high as she spoke. "Hello, again."

"We're back," Jim said, revealing his unforgettable smile.

"It's nice to see both of you," Amanda said calmly. However, she could feel her heart racing a bit, and she knew it was because she was nervous about revealing her idea to them.

They walked into her office and sat down. Karen glanced at the painting still propped on the easel but didn't say anything, which made Amanda wonder if she should have moved it prior to the meeting. She also felt annoyed with herself for not working on it, so she made a secret vow that she would complete it soon.

"Would you like something to drink?" Amanda asked.

"Nothing for me," Jim answered.

Karen shook her head. "Me neither."

"Okay, then. How was your week?" Amanda asked. She sensed that they wanted to get started right away.

Karen's eyes narrowed, and she spoke quickly. "It wasn't quite as bad. I only had the horrible dream about the woman one time this week. I did have a new one, though, in which I was trapped in East Germany before the Berlin Wall came down. I was running from someone, desperately trying to escape, but I don't know who it was. I woke up before I could see the face of the person."

"How did you feel the next morning?"

"It seemed so real that I thought about it all day. However, I didn't feel as bad as I did when I had the nightmare about the woman getting beaten."

"I have a question for both of you," Amanda said cautiously. "Do you know anything about your ancestors—who they were, where they were born, and how they lived?"

Karen and Jim exchanged puzzled looks.

"We don't know a lot about them," Jim answered. "Why do you ask?"

"I have a theory, and it is only a theory at best, mind you. Have you ever heard of behavioral epigenetics or ancestral trauma?"

"No," Jim and Karen replied in unison.

"There have been studies which show that if something traumatic happens to a person, it causes anxiety in future generations. According to scientists, this doesn't mean the descendants remember the incident. There is no proof that people remember the events their ancestors encountered. However, I'm wondering if some inherit a feeling of fear from a specific past event. Perhaps Karen might be dreaming about an ancestor. I know this sounds impossible. I have absolutely no proof of this, but I'm curious if this might be the case in this situation."

Amanda couldn't tell what Jim and Karen were thinking, but by the look on their faces, they appeared to be confused. "So, what are your thoughts?" she asked.

There was an awkward silence, and then Jim spoke. "It does sound weird, but honestly, we'll consider any idea at this point. What do you think, Karen?"

"I agree. It's an odd idea, but I'm open to anything."

Amanda continued. "Here's where I think we should start. Find out your ancestors' names, and then research their lives. There's so much information online about families and their history. I also think it would be good for both of you to take a DNA test to find out more about your heritage. Most of the companies allow you to contact people who are a match to your DNA. Sometimes they have information you don't have on your ancestors. I've done this myself, and I've found distant cousins this way."

"How will this help to find out if any specific fears from our ancestors were passed down to Karen?"

"You might find out some information about their lives and what might have happened to them."

"Hmm. I don't know what we'd find out if we searched deeply into our history," Jim said.

Karen nodded, then said, "And so, if we find out that one of our female ancestors was beaten by a man, then that might be why I'm having the nightmare about it?"

"That might be the reason for it, and you might find out other things about your heredity which might be contributing to your nightmares. I know this is not a definite science, and it does sound like a far reach. I totally understand if you'd like to go back to a psychiatrist or psychologist," Amanda explained.

"I don't want to do that at this point. I think I'll give this a try. It will be interesting to seek out the information, even if it leads to nothing," Karen said.

Jim nodded.

"Well, then. Here are some DNA companies from which to choose," Amanda said. She quickly wrote the company names on a small piece of paper and handed it to Karen. It can take several weeks to get the results, so please be patient. In the meantime, read through any documents you might have, and look through your family Bible if you have one. In my family, someone long ago documented names, birth dates, and death dates, and put the information in a Bible."

"Okay, we'll do it," Jim said, standing up to shake Amanda's hand.

She felt her face flush as they shook hands, and she sensed Jim noticed it by his smile. It was a sly sort of smile paired with an all-knowing look, and she was slightly embarrassed. She most certainly felt an attraction toward him but didn't want to show it. Relationships had never worked out well for her in the past. Amanda knew part of the problem was her tendency to put her career before the people in her life. She barely made time for the men she'd dated in the past, and they eventually got tired of it and walked away. She understood this, so she tried to avoid getting involved. Jim scared her. She'd never been so attracted to anyone before, and she knew her life was about to change. There were no excuses this time. She'd left her job, and she now had time to be with someone and to fall in love. For that reason, Amanda was both petrified and excited. She was jolted from her thoughts as Jim let go of her hand. He continued to smile and looked into her eyes, and she sensed that he might be attracted to her as well. She composed herself and spoke as professionally as she could.

"Remember, there is no charge for today. This was a very quick meeting, and you overpaid me last time."

"If you insist."

"I do."

Karen interrupted. "When should I come back to see you?"

"Are you free on Monday?" Amanda asked. "We'll just keep the time as one o'clock to make it easy, if that works for you."

Karen nodded and said, "Yes, I believe I can do that." She turned to Jim. "Are you free to drive me then? I've been so tired lately that I don't feel comfortable behind the wheel."

"Yes. I will always make time if you need me."

"I'll put it on my calendar and will plan to see you on Monday," Amanda confirmed.

After the Dorions left, her phone buzzed, and she noticed it was Carolyn's name on caller ID.

"Hi, there," Amanda answered.

"How are you and what have you been doing?" Carolyn asked in a tone that Amanda remembered all too well. She knew Carolyn was about to request something of her.

"I had a couple of guests, but they've just left," Amanda responded.

"How would you like to come over this evening at around six o'clock?"

"I believe I can do that. Is anything wrong?"

"No. I'd just like to see you and get you out of the house."

Amanda rolled her eyes, but she kept her voice cheerful. "Sure. I'll see you then."

"Good!"

They ended the call, and she had a strange feeling there was more going on than what was being revealed by her friend.

That evening, as she approached the street in front of Carolyn's house, Amanda wasn't surprised to see a lot of cars in front of the brick bungalow. She could always tell when Carolyn was up to something, and it appeared she was right again. She was certain there were people waiting inside to greet her. She parked her car, took a deep breath, and walked to the front door. Carolyn and her husband, Rod, opened the door, and she was greeted with a flood of people from her past. This was the high school reunion she'd never attended, and she felt slightly nervous. She had never liked being the center of attention.

"So nice to see you!" a male voice shouted.

"It's been over twenty years since we've seen you," a female voice said. Amanda didn't recognize the lady at all.

There were about thirty people in the living room, and they were all converging on her. She cursed Carolyn under her breath, but she knew it was all with good intentions. Slowly, a good-looking man with black curly hair came toward her. She recognized him as Matt, who was the guy she'd always dreamed of being with when she was a teenager. He'd always been nice to her, but they had never dated. Amanda saw that he was still quite handsome. His brown eyes held the same sparkle, and the laugh lines that surrounded them added to their character. She looked down at his left hand and saw a gold wedding band. Matt was most certainly off the market.

"It's so nice to see you, Amanda," he said softly. "I'd always hoped to see you at a high school reunion, but you never came."

"I know. I just never had the time."

"Well, you're here now. Miami County always calls people back, even after years of being away."

"I do feel as if I'm where I belong. Did you leave town, too?"

"I moved to San Diego, where I met my wife. It was hard to convince her to leave California, but the housing prices were so high that she decided to give this move a try. We've been here for ten years now. She does miss the beach and the weather in San Diego, but we go back there every summer with the kids."

"How many kids do you have?"

"We have two boys—10 and 12 years old. Do you have any kids?"

Amanda had always hated this question. She felt as if people judged her for not having any children. "No kids," she answered quickly.

Matt smiled. "Well, take it from me, it's like living in a zoo."

Everyone in the room was watching as they spoke to each other, and then Carolyn stepped forward. "Thanks so much for coming so we can welcome Amanda back to the community! She's been gone much too long. Let's have a good time tonight! My kids are at their grandma's and we're ready to party."

Everyone clapped and shouted, "Welcome home!"

Amanda knew she had to say something, even though public speaking was not one of her strong points. "I'd also like to thank you all for coming," she said, her hands trembling a bit. "I must say that I was very excited when I came through the door this evening. I'm sorry I haven't been back to the reunions. I've always thought of you fondly, and I'm very glad to be here tonight."

"We're glad, too!" a male voice shouted from the group. And with that, there was laughter.

It turned out to be a wonderful evening, and Amanda was grateful to everyone for being there. After the last guest left, she offered to help clean up, but Carolyn wouldn't hear of it. And then, as she drove home, she realized she could never leave this place again.

Chapter Four

Amanda woke up later than usual on Monday morning—at 8:58, to be precise. After pouring a cup of coffee, she put on a fleece jacket and went outside to sit on the deck. Bandy bounded down the stairs to the yard to chase a squirrel. The leaves were nearly gone from the trees, but it was a beautiful sunny morning. Amanda knew her routine of sitting outside would soon have to end when frigid temperatures arrived. This made her a bit sad, as she didn't quite know what to do with herself during the winter—especially now that she wasn't working. She was keenly aware of the fact that it might be time to make a plan for her life. She was becoming restless. Her thoughts turned to the unfinished painting in her office, and she decided that the winter months would be a good time to finish it. Perhaps she'd even start another one.

After drinking several cups of coffee and eating a bowl of oatmeal, Amanda decided to go to her computer to read her email. She had several messages from former co-workers checking in to see if she was ever coming back to the office. She answered each one warmly but stressed that she was happy and wouldn't be returning. However, she knew they wouldn't understand. Her former co-workers were very driven people, but she knew from private conversations with some of them that the long hours and caseloads were overwhelming at times. She always listened intently, but she never revealed her true feelings to anyone there. Maybe that was another reason she became so burned out. She didn't feel comfortable venting to others, so she was worn from carrying the burden.

After answering the emails, Amanda showered and dressed in her most tailored clothes—navy-blue slacks and a blazer. The ensemble made her look very thin. She usually wore baggy clothing, so most people had no idea she had such a tiny waist. After applying a touch of make-up, she decided to eat lunch before Jim and Karen arrived.

As usual, they were prompt. Jim smiled as Amanda opened the door, and she noticed that his gaze ventured from the top of her body to her feet. She assumed the tailored ensemble had caught his eye. She also took notice of what he was wearing—a black pullover sweater tucked into a pair of faded jeans, and he looked quite handsome as usual. She knew that clothes don't make a person, but she had to admit that she liked Jim's casual style.

Karen also smiled, but the dark circles under her eyes revealed that she hadn't slept well.

"Welcome back," Amanda said. "Come on in and sit down. Would you like some water?"

Jim shook his head, and Karen said, "No thanks."

After they were all seated, Jim said, "We've found out some things about our family."

Karen nodded.

"Would you like to tell me about it?" Amanda asked.

Karen answered. "We've found information which has proven to be disturbing on many levels."

"How so?"

Karen glanced at Jim as if she wanted him to speak for her, but he didn't take the bait. Amanda was pleased about that. It was good for her to find her own voice.

Karen sighed deeply and continued, and Amanda noticed that her hands were steady. "We found a piece of paper that had the names of our family members written on it. Birth and death dates were also written beside some of the names. The page was folded inside an old German Bible that had been in a closet in our maternal grandmother's home. We took the Bible after she passed away, but we also put it in a closet and never looked through it until now. We searched online for information about a few of the names we found. In one instance, we learned of a disturbing court case that was featured in several newspaper articles. The court case was about our great-great-grandmother Margarethe Mueller. She was a German immigrant, who came to Illinois in the late 1800s, and she was beaten severely by her first husband—so much so that she nearly died. This man was not our great-great-grandfather, whom she married later."

It was then that Karen's hands started shaking, and tears began to roll down her cheeks. She looked at Jim for help, and then pulled a tissue from her purse. Amanda nodded at Jim to let him know it was okay to finish the story.

He continued where she left off. "The court case and newspaper articles we found about Margarethe provided some graphic details of the beating she took from her husband. His name was Karl Brinkmann, and it's fortunate they had no children. The beating happened in 1870, and the trial took place in 1871. No one has ever mentioned this history to us, so you can imagine how surprised we were to discover it. We know from the court document that Margarethe was granted a divorce from Karl, and he was sentenced to prison. Margarethe then married our great-great-grandfather Hans Mueller, and they had several children, including our great-grandfather Johann.

Unfortunately, Karl was released from prison early, because several people from the community wrote letters to the governor on his behalf."

Amanda shook her head. "Anything else?"

"Yes. Margarethe's name was written inside the front cover of our German Bible. The dates next to her name indicated that she was born in April of 1846 and died in January of 1895. Hans's name was written at the bottom of the page without any dates. We can't find a burial record for either of them, so it will be hard to find additional information. We once heard that our great-grandfather Johann and his siblings were abandoned and raised by a minister. That's all we know about the family."

Amanda didn't know what to say. Jim and Karen were staring at her, waiting for her response. She finally spoke.

"I know this must be shocking to both of you, and you might be wishing you had never unleashed this secret. However, I believe it's important to learn this history." She looked at Karen. "It could be a coincidence that you are dreaming of a woman being beaten, but it is indeed interesting. Have you had the nightmare since learning about your great-great-grandmother?"

"Yes. I had the nightmare last night," Karen answered quickly.

Jim said, "We tried to find Margarethe on the cemetery website where most of our Mueller family members are listed as being buried, but her name isn't there. Hans isn't listed either."

"Did you talk to anyone in the cemetery business office?" Amanda asked.

"Yes. I called, but the man who works there said there's no record of them. By the way, the cemetery is in Hillsdale, Kansas. After immigrating to Illinois from Germany, our ancestors also lived there for a while."

"Hillsdale isn't far from here," Amanda said. "Maybe you should go there to see for yourself."

"I don't believe we need to know where they're buried," Karen said. "I think we just need to know what happened to them."

"I agree, but perhaps finding their graves would provide additional insight," Amanda offered.

Karen nodded.

Amanda continued. "I also think you'll need to find out if any of your great-grandfather's siblings had children and research their information. Maybe you'll find something about Margarethe that way. You should be able to search for them online."

"Sure, we can do that," Jim said. "I agree that going to the cemetery would provide extra insight—if that's okay with Karen. We'll also be able to see the graves of our other ancestors. We've never done that before."

"I'm okay with that," Karen said. "I just wanted to stress that knowing what happened to them in life is more important than where they might be buried."

"I understand," Amanda said. "I'm hopeful Margarethe's grave might be there, even though it's not listed on the database. Maybe her information is missing from the records. We can only hope because that would eliminate the possibility that she returned to Germany. It would be difficult to search for information in another country. Do you know if she might have had a nickname that would have been on the headstone instead? Perhaps the man in the cemetery office couldn't find records because she's under a different name. I say this because my own German ancestors changed the spelling of their names."

"I'll check," Karen said.

Jim looked at Amanda. "Would you like to go with us to the cemetery?"

Amanda wasn't expecting to be invited to come along, and she knew it might go against protocol. However, this was no ordinary case, and she was no longer working in a clinic. And so, she decided to accept the offer. "I'd love to go with you."

"Good," Jim said, smiling.

"It will be nice to have you with us," Karen added. "We can go right now if you're free, and you can consider it as part of the session."

Jim nodded.

"Sure. I just need to take out the dog before we leave."

"Great!" Jim said. "You can ride with us. We'll wait for you in the car."

After taking care of Bandy, Amanda grabbed her purse and went out the front door, locking it behind her. As she got into the back seat of the car, she noticed it was spotless. *Everything about Jim was perfect,* she thought.

They arrived at the cemetery about twenty minutes later and parked in the graveled lot. It was a well-kept property with a stone chapel and business office. There was only one other car parked there—a white Honda Civic.

"We need to go to the north side where the stones are older," Jim said. "That's where the Mueller family is buried."

They got out of the car and began walking northward on a gravel road. Amanda noticed a change in the stones as they slowly reached the older section. Some were crooked, and their chiseled writing was hard to read.

"Do either of you know Margarethe's maiden name?' Amanda asked.

Karen looked puzzled. "I don't. Do you know, Jim?"

"I think it might have been Schminke. Why do you ask?"

"Perhaps she's listed under her maiden name," Amanda replied.

"It's worth a look," Jim said, walking swiftly toward a row of headstones situated under a large Maple tree. "Here's the Mueller area," he announced.

They went to each stone and studied it, not saying a word to one another until Amanda broke the silence. "Do any of the names look familiar to you?"

"Here's the grave of our great-grandfather Johann, which is next to the headstone of our great-grandmother Fredericka," Karen said, pointing.

"And here's the grave for our great-great-uncle Ernst," Jim said, motioning toward another nearby stone. "I see other Mueller graves, but I don't recognize the names."

"That's odd," Karen said, motioning toward an empty space. "It looks like someone has been buried there, but there's no headstone."

"You're right," Amanda agreed.

Jim stopped and observed the space. "Maybe the stone was old and broken, so someone took it away. Hard to know for sure though," he said, and then began walking again.

They continued to observe the stones, but there was no Margarethe Mueller, nor the surname of Schminke to be found.

"Let's go to the business office to see if there's anyone there who might be able to provide us with some answers," Amanda suggested.

Jim nodded. "Sounds like a good idea."

They turned and walked down the gravel path toward the office. Jim stepped up to the door first and then tapped lightly, while Karen and Amanda stood behind him. An elderly man wearing glasses and a pair of overalls appeared seconds later.

"May I help you?" the man asked. He had sparkling blue eyes that seemed to dance with excitement as he eyed his visitors.

"I hope so. My name is Jim Dorion. I'm here with my sister, Karen, and our friend, Amanda Latham. Karen and I would like to ask about a family member who might be buried somewhere in this cemetery."

"Certainly. Come on inside. My name is Hank Autin, by the way."

As they walked inside, Amanda noticed the walls were lined with shelves and filled with antiques and books. There was a large table in the middle of the room with an old black typewriter sitting on it. The only thing that appeared to be from the present-day was a computer on a counter. Hank walked behind the counter and stood next to the computer. "What's the name?" he asked.

"Margarethe Mueller," Jim answered quickly.

"She might also be listed as Margarethe Schminke," Karen added.

"German, eh," Hank stated, keying in the names. "Well, there are several people with the name of Mueller, but I don't see a Margarethe. Someone called here recently and asked about her as well."

"That was me," Jim admitted. "I believed you, but I thought we'd come take a look for ourselves anyway."

"Is there anyone with the last name of Schminke buried here?" Amanda asked.

"Not that I see," Hank responded.

"What about Hans Mueller? Do you see that name at all?" Jim asked.

Hank typed the name, and then said, "No one by that name buried here either, I'm afraid."

"Okay. Thank you very much," Karen said, sounding disappointed.

"Is there anything else I can help you with?"

"Yes, there's one more thing," Karen answered. "I noticed there might be a missing headstone in the Mueller section. Would you have a record of that?"

"It should be listed in the database," Hank answered, adjusting his glasses as he typed. "Ah, here's the information on that. There has never been a headstone, but Sophia Mueller Johnson is buried there."

"That is sad," Jim said, frowning. "I remember seeing her name listed on the family information page we found in the Bible, but nothing was written about her. She was our great-great-aunt."

"Does the database have her birth date listed?" Karen asked.

"It says that she was born in 1882 and died in 1902."

"Wow. She was only 20 years old," Jim said.

"It's hard to believe the family didn't honor her life with a headstone," Karen said.

Hank frowned as he shook his head. "I'm afraid that was the case sometimes. There were families who couldn't afford it—there still are. I've seen this before."

"Thanks for your help," Jim said, turning to walk out the door.

Amanda and Karen followed close behind him.

"Good luck to you," Hank called. "I hope you find the people you're searching for."

"We do, too," Karen said.

"Well, that was a dead-end," Jim remarked as they walked to the car.

Karen nudged his arm. "That's not the thing to say in a cemetery!"

"I didn't mean it like that. Sorry. This was a waste of time though."

"Actually, it wasn't," Amanda disagreed. "You now know for sure that neither Margarethe nor Hans are buried here."

"You're right," Jim acknowledged, clicking his key fob to unlock the car doors.

Karen sighed as she got inside. "Oh, well. It was worth a try."

"This just means you'll need to do more research. I can help if you'd like," Amanda offered.

"We'd love that," Jim answered quickly.

Amanda noticed he was grinning at her in the rearview mirror. She returned the smile and noticed a definite twinkle in his eyes. It was as if he knew she was attracted to him, and he seemed quite pleased by it.

Hank waited until their car was out of the parking lot before he made a phone call. He'd noticed something else written on the database file besides the date of birth and death for Sophia Mueller Johnson—something that indicated he was to discreetly call a certain phone number if anyone ever came to inquire about the woman. Hank didn't know with whom he'd be speaking, and he didn't understand why he was supposed to make the call. However, the instructions were rather strange. He was supposed to enter the code number *1882* after he was connected, but that was the extent of the information provided. After two rings, an automated voice said to submit the code. Hank carefully entered *1882,* suddenly realizing it was the year Sophia was born. Several seconds later, a live male voice said, "You have entered the code for Sophia Mueller Johnson. Is this correct?"

"Yes, sir. What's this about?"

The man said, "I need to know if someone requested information about the woman."

"Yes, they did."

"Who were they?"

"They were Sophia's relatives. I believe their names were Jim and Karen Dorion. They also brought a friend, but I can't remember her name."

"No matter. It's the family members that I need to know about."

"Why? Are you related to them?"

"Let's just say I'm related to them in a most unfortunate way. It's important that facts don't get twisted. I need to know what you told them about Sophia's death," the man replied.

"I just gave them the dates of her birth and death."

"Good. That's all there is to know, I'm afraid. Did they ask about any other members of the Mueller family?"

"Yes," Hank answered hesitantly. "They asked about Margarethe and Hans Mueller, but there is no record of them being buried here. That's why they came to the cemetery office in the first place."

The man was quiet for a second. "I see. Thanks for the information. Please call me if they ever return to ask about the woman or any of the other Mueller family members, for that matter."

"Of course, but I still don't understand why I needed to call you. I've never seen anything like this in the database before today."

"It does not concern you. Thank you for calling."

"Sure," Hank said, frowning. "By the way, what's your name?" He wasn't sure he'd done the right thing by calling the man, and he had a bad feeling in the pit of his stomach.

"My name is not important at this time. One more thing though. If you ever see those people again, do not tell them about this phone call or you won't like the consequences. Good-bye," the man said, clicking off his phone. He then made a call of his own. "Simon, this is Senator Bart Kleiner. We might have a potential problem..."

Hank felt uneasy after the phone call, and he wasn't sure what he should do. He wondered if he should talk to the police about it, but he instead decided to go see his friend, Debbie Blake, to let her know what happened.

Chapter Five

The ride back to Amanda's home was filled with conversation about how to research what happened to Margarethe and Hans. They all agreed to search on their own and then get together in a few days to go over what they had found. Karen confessed to being nervous about going to sleep that night because she didn't want to have another nightmare. She also wanted to learn more about Margarethe.

After arriving at Amanda's, Jim and Karen decided to leave without coming inside.

Jim rolled down his window after she stepped out of the car. "We'll start researching as soon as possible," he said.

"Good luck," Amanda said, leaning toward the window. "I have names now, so I'll get started on it, too."

"Thank you," Karen said.

"Call me if you need to talk," Amanda offered. "Otherwise, why don't you come back on Friday at noon to discuss what we've found."

Jim glanced at Karen, who quickly nodded. He then said, "Sure, that would be great."

As Amanda looked into his eyes and felt her attraction growing, she knew it was time to excuse herself from working with Karen on a professional level. "I was thinking," she said slowly. "If you remember, I didn't want to take on any clients, and I still don't. I'd like to help you as a friend at this point. Would that be okay?"

Jim's eyes widened. "Are you sure?" We're prepared to pay you."

"Yes. I'm sure. This is turning out to be a case like none I've ever handled. Since I'm very interested in learning about ancestral trauma and how it plays out with descendants, I believe this is a learning experience from which I'll benefit. I don't feel right charging for that." She was rambling, trying to make up an excuse that would sound reasonable. She knew her feelings for Jim would make it unethical to be Karen's therapist. Even though he wasn't technically her client, he was involved with the case.

"Okay, if you insist," Jim said, sounding rather disappointed.

She couldn't tell if he was worried that she might walk away from the case, or if he was insulted in some manner. "I'll see you on Friday," she assured.

Jim smiled and nodded as he put the car in reverse. Amanda waved and turned to walk inside. She wondered if Karen had noticed the attraction yet. She hoped not. That would be a distraction for her while she was trying to figure out her family's past.

Amanda awoke early the next morning after again having the dream of riding the black horse through the lush green field. She was humming to herself as she thought of it. The man in the dream definitely looked like Jim. The two horses trotted around each other as usual, but this time they stopped. Both riders dismounted and walked toward each other until they were standing face-to-face. They reached out and held each other in a tight embrace and kissed so passionately that Amanda didn't want to wake up. But she did—right in the middle of it. She could almost feel Jim's arms around her as she opened her eyes, which was a wonderful way to start the day.

As the reality of life set in, Amanda remembered she needed to work on the family research for Karen and Jim. Although the internet was a good source for information, she also knew there were many things that weren't true. She decided to gather as much as possible from an online search, and then validate it with records or newspaper articles. That was her hope, anyway. She typed the name, *Sophia Mueller Johnson*, then added, *born 1882*. Although the search returned with nothing about Sophia, it did provide a link to an international genealogy website. Amanda quickly clicked on it. There was a white box displayed with a prompt to show where to type an individual's name for the search. She keyed it in carefully. *Sophia Mueller Johnson* was found in the database, and her information instantly appeared. Amanda first checked the dates and burial place to make sure they matched. They were correct. The website indicated that Sophia was born in 1882 and died in 1902, and that she was buried in Hillsdale, Kansas. The site listed her parents as Margarethe and Hans Mueller, so there was no doubt the data was correct. She was married to a man named Thomas Johnson. Amanda was interrupted when her phone buzzed. Because the caller ID displayed Carolyn's name and number, she answered the call.

"Hi, Carolyn. How are you?"

"I'm fine, but the kids have been sick. Luckily, Rod and I haven't caught it yet."

"Glad you haven't, but I'm sorry about the kids."

"There's always something going on in this house. It's never boring, that's for sure. And so, enough mindless chit-chat. What have you been doing?"

"I decided to take on a client, and I've been meeting with her," Amanda confessed, purposely leaving Jim out of the equation. She didn't want Carolyn to start asking questions that she wasn't ready to answer.

Carolyn sighed. "I knew you couldn't live out your days tending to your garden and selling produce. Of course, you can't really be doing that now, since we're deep into fall."

"My old office in the city gave out my information and referred the individual to me. I didn't seek it, and I didn't want to take on a client at this point. Now that I did, though, I'm glad to be back in the field at a much slower pace. I saw too many clients each day in the city, and it was draining. It wasn't fair to them either."

"Well, I think this town is lucky to have you here, and I know of some who might set up an appointment if you decide to go into full-practice mode again."

"I don't know about that yet, but I'll certainly let you know if I do."

"Okay, then. I'd better go check on the kids. Don't be a stranger."

"Good to talk to you," Amanda said before disconnecting the call. She knew she wouldn't be able to keep Jim a secret from Carolyn very long.

Amanda returned to the computer to research Sophia. She found a newspaper article, which indicated that the police were called to the home because Sophia's husband had abused her. She read the story a couple of times, feeling deep sadness for the woman. She again clicked on the genealogy website to see if she could find any burial information on Margarethe and Hans. Unfortunately, there was nothing in that regard, but the newspaper articles about Margarethe's beating popped up. Amanda quickly read each one but found the details to be the same as Karen and Jim described, so she gained no further insight. Frustrated, she decided to stop searching. *It would be best*, she thought, *to wait to see what the Dorions found in their own research.* Besides, she felt like it was time to lighten her mood by watching funny videos. Her favorites featured people's pets doing silly things, so she clicked on a few of those. There was a new one with a chicken on a swing, twirling around and then gliding back and forth. Amanda smiled and moved on to the next video featuring a pig pushing a ball with its nose through a field. The next video made her laugh out loud though, as it displayed an English bulldog riding a skateboard with a calico cat on its back, and they appeared to be enjoying the ride.

On Friday morning, Amanda took extra time in getting ready. She carefully picked out her most flattering pair of jeans, which she paired with a crisp, no-iron white blouse. She loved no-iron blouses. They always looked starched, but they were soft enough to be comfortable. It was a chilly morning, so she chose to wear a fitted black wool blazer to complete the outfit. She then went to her computer to respond to emails. As she read more messages from her old office, she sighed out loud. Some of her former colleagues were still trying to get her to return. She again answered them graciously, stating that she was very content with the decision she'd made to leave.

At a quarter of twelve, Amanda heard Jim's car pull into the driveway. She straightened some paperwork on her desk before the Dorions rang the bell. Bandy barked once as they entered the house, but then rolled over on the rug for a belly rub. Jim quickly obliged.

"She must like you," Amanda said. She was happy about that because she believed dogs were good judges of character.

"I love dogs," Jim said, smiling.

"Do you have one?"

"Not at this time. We used to have a Jack Russell terrier, and I hope to get another one soon. I really miss Jack."

"His name was Jack?"

"Yes. I know that isn't very original," Jim said, grinning.

Karen snickered. "That dog was a real character. He stole our socks and hid them throughout the house. To this day, I think I'm missing a pair!"

"Pets do add humor to our lives," Amanda said, smiling. She was glad to witness Karen's lightheartedness. "Is it okay if I keep Bandy here with us since you're now friends?"

Jim nodded. "Absolutely."

Bandy followed them into the office and plopped down on the rug for a nap. They all sat down to discuss what they'd found in their research.

"How are you?" Amanda asked.

Karen answered. "We're doing okay, but I had the nightmare again."

"I'm sorry," Amanda said. She noticed that Jim appeared to be concerned. His lips were tightly clamped together, and his eyes were focused intently on Karen. "Are you okay, Jim?"

"I'm fine, but I still hate it that she's going through this."

"It's not your fault," Karen said gently.

"Do you feel like talking about it now?" Amanda asked. "We can also discuss anything you might have found in your research if you'd rather do that first."

"Let's discuss the research," Karen responded.

Amanda nodded. "Sure. By the way, did either of you take one of the DNA tests that I mentioned?"

"We ordered the kits but haven't received them yet," Jim answered.

"You might be able to connect with distant relatives that way, and they might have more information," Amanda said, and then changed the subject. "What have you learned through your research?"

Jim nodded. "Okay, so there were only a couple of Margarethe's children who survived into adulthood and had children of their own."

"Oh, I didn't realize that," Amanda said, disappointed. "It's still worth looking into though. It only takes one relative with information who's willing to share it."

"I agree," Karen said. "And even if we don't find out anything, it would still be interesting to find distant cousins. I really want to learn more about Margarethe though."

Jim nodded. "It's not going to hurt to keep searching."

"What were the names of Margarethe's kids who survived into adulthood and had children?" Amanda asked.

"Margarethe and Hans had four children—Ernst, Sophia, Albrecht, and our great-grandfather Johann. Ernst and Johann survived and had children. Albrecht was killed in World War I, and he's buried in France. We're fairly certain Sophia had no children, because none are listed in the family Bible," Jim said.

"So, the Mueller section we saw at the cemetery was for the family of Ernst, Sophia, and your great-grandparents, right?" Amanda questioned.

"That's correct," Karen answered.

"Where are your grandparents buried?"

"They're in the Paola, Kansas, cemetery. Their names were Friedrich and Anna Rohr," Jim replied.

"Hmm," Amanda said. "I just thought of something. I found an international genealogy website and searched for burial information on Hans and Margrethe, but I couldn't find anything. Maybe we should specifically check Paola's website just in case it wasn't listed on the international link."

"I hadn't thought of that," Karen responded. "It's worth a look."

Amanda went to her desk and pulled out the computer keyboard. Karen and Jim followed and stood behind her as she clicked on the monitor. As the screen came to life, the last scene in the video of the skateboarding dog and cat was still visible. She'd forgotten to close the link.

"What's that?" Jim asked as he nudged Karen and laughed.

Amanda felt slightly embarrassed. "Oh, that's just a funny video I was watching."

"Can we see it?" Karen asked.

"I know I'd like to," Jim said, grinning.

"You're serious?"

Karen nodded, and Jim said, "Absolutely."

Amanda clicked on the arrow to start the video, and the dog and cat could be seen rolling down a street. The large English bulldog used its right front paw to push on the ground to keep the skateboard going, while the cat clung to its back.

"Well, that's something you don't see every day," Jim remarked, still grinning.

"Very funny," Karen said.

Amanda smiled and nodded. "Okay, I guess we should get down to business now," she said, clicking the *close* tab on the link. She then found the Paola cemetery website. Although it was unlikely that Margarethe would be listed under her maiden name, she keyed in *Schminke* just in case. The results came back with zero matches. She then typed *Mueller,* but there weren't any matches for that surname either. Since Karen and Jim were certain their grandma and grandpa Rohr were buried in Paola, she typed their surname to find out whether the website was accurate. The information for Friedrich and Anna Rohr popped into view.

"That's our grandparents," Jim acknowledged. "Our grandma Anna was the only child of our great-grandfather Johann Mueller."

"Okay, so we know the site is accurate," Amanda said. "I believe we should now focus on Margarethe's other son, Ernst. Were the names of his kids listed in the family Bible?"

Karen nodded, and then walked to her chair and picked up her purse. "I actually have a copy of the page in my purse," she said, pulling out a folded sheet of paper.

"That's perfect," Amanda said. "You're welcome to sit at my computer to search the names if you'd like."

"Sure."

Amanda got up and stood next to Jim while Karen took the chair. He turned toward her and briefly smiled, and she returned the gesture. She realized she didn't know much about Jim's past, except that his parents died when he was 22 years old, and he worked in the information technology field. He'd never mentioned being married before, nor that he had any children. She didn't feel comfortable asking about it either.

Before Karen began typing, Amanda felt she should mention what she found out about Margarethe's daughter. "Before you search for Ernst, there's something I'd like to tell you about Sophia."

Karen turned around. "What did you find out?"

"She was married to a man named Thomas Johnson, and the police were called to the house because he abused her."

"That is horrible," Jim said, shaking his head. "Sophia was abused by her husband just like her mother."

Karen sighed heavily. "So much violence."

Chapter 6

Karen appeared to be calm and her hands were steady as she positioned them on the computer keyboard. However, Amanda thought it was a good time to find out how she was feeling before they began the search for Ernst Mueller. "How are you doing?" she asked.

Karen turned in her chair and looked up at her. "I'm learning to cope, and I believe you've helped me with that. You've never treated me like I'm a freak. It's as if you truly understand."

"I'm glad you feel that way. And you're not a freak, by the way."

Karen blushed. "Thank you."

Jim glanced at Amanda and nodded.

"Okay, then, let's get this search going," Karen said, turning around to face the computer.

"I think we should still use the international genealogy website," Amanda said, leaning over Karen's shoulder. "I saved it as a favorite. You can click on it on the right side of the screen."

Karen clicked on the site and then typed, *Ernst Mueller.* The results were quickly received. Ernst had three kids. Their names were Heinrich, Wilhelm, and Catherine, which were the same names listed on the page from the family Bible. This excited Karen, as she clapped a hand over her mouth and gasped. "Wow, this is cool! I'll now try Heinrich."

The name appeared as quickly as the others, and the site indicated that Heinrich was buried in Hillsdale,

Kansas. However, Amanda didn't remember seeing his grave when they were there. He was born in 1918 and died in 1998. He was the father of Phillip and Maddie Mueller. Phillip was born in 1942, and since no date of death was mentioned, it appeared that he was still living. Maddie was born in 1943, but she died in 1973.

"Go ahead and print that page," Amanda directed. "We might be able to find Phillip if the site is up to date and he's really still alive. It's easier to find men anyway, since they normally don't change their last names when they get married."

Karen then typed the second name. Wilhelm was born in 1920, and he was the father of two children. Their names were Caroline and Ava, and they were both born in the 1940s.

"I doubt we'll be able to locate them, since they probably have different married names," Amanda said.

"Should I still look up Catherine, then?" Karen asked.

"Yes. Go ahead."

Catherine Mueller came up as Catherine Mueller Jones.

"We probably won't find anything further on Catherine," Jim said. "Jones is such a common name." And indeed, there was nothing more.

"You can join a heritage group later if we don't find Phillip Mueller," Amanda said. "Sometimes different websites have more information, but a few of them charge a fee."

She then pointed at the monitor. "Let's do a search for Phillip now to see if anything pops up, but don't use the genealogy website for that. Just do a general search."

Several links came up about Phillip Mueller as soon as Karen finished typing his name. The links all led to the same person. Phillip was listed as living in Kansas City, and he was a retired teacher.

Karen grinned. "He's local. We have a relative nearby that we never knew about!"

"Now, what do we do?" Jim asked.

"We can contact him," Amanda said. "His phone number is also listed."

Jim sighed. "It's rather scary that everyone's information can be so easily accessed these days."

"Yes, it is. I don't like it, but in this case, it's a good thing," Amanda said.

"That's true," Karen agreed.

"So, do you want to call him now?" Amanda asked.

"Why not," Jim shrugged. He looked at Karen, who nodded in agreement.

"Will you talk to him first?" she asked.

"Sure," he answered, pulling his phone from his pocket. He then punched in the number and put the phone on speaker.

A woman answered hesitantly. "Hello?"

"Hello, my name is Jim Dorion, and I'm a descendant of the Mueller family. Are you related to Phillip Mueller, by chance?"

"Phillip is my husband, and I answered his phone. Would you like to speak with him?"

"That would be great."

"Sure. Hold on a minute. He stepped outside."

Within a couple of minutes, a male voice came through the speaker. "Hello, this is Phillip Mueller."

"Thanks for taking my call. My name is Jim Dorion, and I'm a descendant of the Mueller family on my mother's side. My sister, Karen, and I are doing research on their history, and we've reached a roadblock of sorts. I have you on speakerphone, so

Karen can hear, too. Are you the son of Heinrich Mueller, who was the son of Ernst?"

"Yes, I am."

"Ernst was our great-great-uncle," Jim continued. "He was the brother of Johann, who was our great-grandfather. Our research indicates they were the sons of Margarethe and Hans."

"I do remember that my grandpa Ernst had a brother named Johann," Phillip said slowly. "I know that Johann and my grandpa were the only kids who survived well into adulthood and had children of their own. They also had a brother named Albrecht and a sister named Sophia. I know that Albrecht was killed during World War I and is buried in France. My family records indicate that Sophia was killed by her husband."

"Oh, wow!" Karen interrupted. "We went to the cemetery where she's buried, but there wasn't much information about her."

"I have my grandpa's journal, and he wrote that Sophia confided in him that her husband, Thomas Johnson, had threatened to kill her. He was also beating her daily. My grandpa talked to Thomas and told him he'd better lay off her or he'd beat the tar out of him. He also told Sophia to leave and come live with him. She died the next day. Grandpa confronted Thomas at the funeral and got him to confess that he forced her to drink poison. He said no one would believe he did it. Thomas came from a wealthy family and was well thought of in the community. He was right when he said that no one would believe he killed his wife. The police nearly laughed at my grandpa when he reported what Thomas had confessed. It was a different time, and sadly, battered women didn't have much of a voice."

"That's horrible! There isn't even a headstone on Sophia's grave," Jim said. "We're also curious about what you might know about Margarethe and Hans. Karen and I are trying to piece together what became of them. We recently uncovered something horrible that happened to Margarethe—that she was brutally attacked and nearly killed by her former husband. We know that she later married Hans Mueller."

There was silence.

"Are you still there?" Jim asked.

"Yes, I'm here," Phillip said, nearly whispering.

"I'm sorry. I didn't mean to shock you."

Phillip sighed. "You didn't. I know about that. It's just sad that this family went through so much."

Karen's eyes widened with surprise, and Jim seemed perplexed as to what to say. There was again silence for a few seconds.

"Did your grandfather tell you about it?" Jim finally asked.

"Yes, and so did my father. Margarethe never fully recovered from the beating she took. She suffered from severe headaches, depression, and anxiety. Hans handled a lot of the household chores to ease his wife's load. Grandpa Ernst said that his parents always seemed stressed, and they were very watchful of the children. He also said that he once heard them talking about someone threatening to kill them. Not long after that, the family moved from Illinois to Hillsdale, Kansas, and that's when things took a turn for the worse. Margarethe's depressive mood became so bad that she'd spend hours in her bed crying. My grandpa noticed that his father was becoming even more watchful and leery of strangers. One day, a man came to the door, and Hans yelled at him to get off his property. The man spit on him before turning to leave. Hans ran after him and hit him in the mouth. The man punched back, but Hans quickly punched him in the nose. My grandpa was watching all of this from the window, and he said it looked like the man's nose was broken. He ran away and got into a horse-drawn wagon, which was parked on the side of the dirt road."

"Wow! What happened next?" Jim interrupted.

Phillip continued. "Grandpa Ernst said that Hans came into the house and walked straight back to the bedroom where Margarethe sat crying on the bed. Hans shouted that they had been found and it was time to leave. Margarethe sobbed loudly. Grandpa was young, and he didn't understand what was going on, but he knew his life was about to change. He just didn't know how drastic and devastating it would be."

"And then what happened?" Jim prodded.

Phillip sighed. "Grandpa said that things seemed better the next day, because Margarethe wasn't in the bedroom crying. Instead, she was tidying up the house and folding clothes. Hans appeared to be waiting for someone though, because he kept looking out the front window. Finally, in the late afternoon, a preacher by the name of Reverend Kaefer, came to the front door. Hans and Margarethe led him back to the bedroom and shut the door behind them. Of course, my grandpa and his siblings were trying to hear what the adults were talking about, but they were whispering. Finally, the preacher left. Nothing was said about the visit. Grandpa said that his mother and father hugged each kid before tucking them into bed that night. They also told the kids they loved them, which was unusual. This was not a very affectionate family. Grandpa went to sleep thinking that the preacher had come to help his mom, but it was more than that, as he would discover the next morning."

"What happened the next day?" Karen asked.

"Well, that was the day Margarethe and Hans disappeared. My grandpa and his siblings woke up to find that their parents were missing. They searched the house, and then they went outside and looked everywhere. The horses and covered wagon were missing, too. At first, they thought their parents had gone to town to do some shopping and had forgotten to leave a note. A couple of hours went by, and they were becoming confused and distraught. It was then that Reverend Kaefer returned. The kids answered the door, and he told them the news that would forever change their lives. Margarethe and Hans had left town and would not be returning. They were leaving the children to live with him for as long as it was necessary. This was for the children's safety. The kids were understandably quite upset, and a lot of tears were shed that day. Reverend Kaefer told them to gather their things and come with him. My grandpa wasn't sure what to believe at first. He pulled his siblings aside and told them to go ahead and pack their things but to plan on coming home soon. It wasn't that he thought the preacher was fabricating things—he just hoped beyond all hope that his parents would be coming home. Reverend Kaefer tried to explain the situation to the children in a way they could understand. He told them that their parents feared for their lives, due to death threats made against them by some evil men. The only way to protect the children was for their parents to leave so the men would follow them—leading them away from the kids. Reverend Kaefer said that eventually their parents would be able to write letters to them, but for now, everyone needed to remain in hiding without any contact with one another. My grandpa was very upset that Margarethe and Hans didn't explain why they were leaving. Reverend Kaefer said that it was because they were afraid the kids would try to follow them. He assured my grandpa and his siblings that their parents loved them more than words could ever express. Margarethe and Hans had sacrificed everything to keep them safe."

"That is so sad," Karen said. "I can't believe we've never heard about it, but maybe it was because our great-grandpa Johann died before we were born. It seems, though, that his daughter—our grandmother—would have known something about it."

"She probably did know something," Jim said. "Remember, Grandma told us that her father was abandoned. She didn't give details though."

"Oh, yeah. That's right."

"Might I interject here for a moment," Phillip said. "Perhaps your grandmother didn't know the details. Maybe your great-grandfather never told her because he had been so conditioned to secrecy on the matter."

"Interesting," Karen said. "However, we'll never know for sure since everyone is gone. Did your grandpa Ernst tell you anything else about their life with the preacher?"

"Oh, yes, he did," Phillip responded. "Grandpa said that he was a good man, and all of the kids loved him dearly. Together, they built a church in Hillsdale, but it was unfortunately torn down in recent years. Reverend Kaefer never got married and had kids of his own. He devoted his life to Margarethe and Hans's kids. They went to school, played in the creek, fished, farmed, and went to church. It was an ideal life to someone looking in from the outside—rural America at its finest. But the children desperately missed their parents. The pain never went away."

"Did the children ever receive a letter from Margarethe and Hans?" Karen asked.

"They never received anything, but my grandpa found a letter written to Reverend Kaefer that was hidden in a drawer. I'll tell you about that in a minute," Phillip replied. "Keep in mind that my grandpa didn't provide a lot of this information until he was quite old. When my father was growing up, Grandpa told him about Margarethe and how she'd been severely beaten. He never revealed anything else, but my dad always wondered why he was over-protective and somewhat paranoid about strangers. My dad didn't know the extent of the family history until Grandpa was elderly and asked us to come over one day to talk about it. Grandpa said that he wanted us to know the truth about his family, but I believe it was more than that. He seemed to be warning us about something. He said that even though the original people who threatened them were dead and gone, their descendants might carry on the vendetta. He also said that he'd always been watchful for signs of danger, and he now felt it was necessary for someone else to be on alert—either my father or me."

"Wait a minute," Jim interrupted. "There's no way that could be true. I mean, what kind of a family would carry on such a thing? Were they part of a mafia?"

"I know it sounds odd," Phillip agreed. "I'm just repeating what my grandpa told us. My dad and I looked at each other and smiled as he spoke. He picked up on it and accused us of patronizing him, so I know he was of sound mind at the time of the conversation. I haven't felt threatened by anyone during my life though, so I really don't believe there is some family out there with a vendetta against mine. And even if there were, I don't see the point—especially after all these years."

"I don't see the point either," Jim agreed.

"Now, I'll tell you about the letter my grandpa found," Phillip continued. "He said that one day he was looking for something in a drawer at the preacher's house, and he found a folded piece of paper. Curiosity got to him, so he read it. It was a letter from his father to Reverend Kaefer, and it revealed devastating news. Hans had written that Margarethe was missing—that a witness saw a man by the name of Albert Kleiner push her off a river bluff, and she was presumed to be dead. Hans also said that the Kleiner family had a vendetta against Margarethe's family when they all lived in Germany. It had something to do with a dispute over land. Albert had also made advances toward Margarethe and she pushed him away, which made him furious. Hans asked for Reverend Kaefer to continue taking care of the children, because he feared that bringing them to Illinois would put them in danger. He said that he was being threatened daily, because he turned in Albert Kleiner to the police. Nothing had been done about it because Margarethe's body had not been found. Hans indicated that he had confronted Albert Kleiner, but the man denied pushing her into the river. They got into a fight, but it was broken up by some of the other men in the community. Those men also threatened to kill the children if they ever found them. Grandpa was so upset after reading the letter that he ran to the church to talk to Reverend Kaefer. He comforted my grandpa and asked him to keep the letter a secret. He didn't want the other children to know their mother was missing and presumed to be dead until he talked to them—which he did later that day. Grandpa kept the letter, and it was tucked inside his journal when I received it."

"Would you be willing to give us a copy of the letter?" Jim asked.

"I can do that," Phillip replied. "Do you want me to mail it?"

"Sure," Jim said, and then quickly provided the address. "Thank you so much."

"Yes, thanks," Karen said.

"No problem at all. I'm glad you found me. It's great to connect with relatives I've never known. We should meet for lunch or dinner sometime."

Jim said, "We'd like that."

Karen raised her index finger and nodded at Jim, as if she wanted to add something before the call was finished. "Phillip," she said, "do you know if the family home in Hillsdale is still standing?"

"Unfortunately, it is not. There's one more thing. My grandpa never found out what became of Hans. I've searched, but I can't find any records about him. Will you keep me posted on what you find out?"

"We most certainly will do that," Jim answered. "By the way, do you know where Margarethe is buried?"

"I don't think her body was ever recovered from the river."

"That's awful," Jim said, shaking his head.

"Yes, it is. The whole situation had quite an impact on my grandpa. He was a nervous man and often seemed to be depressed."

Karen grimaced. "Did anyone else in your family suffer from anxiety or depression?"

"My sister had a lot of anxiety while we were growing up. My dad was rather moody and high-tempered, so I always thought that his moods made her stressed," Phillip explained.

"I have a lot of anxiety myself."

"I'm sorry to hear that."

"I'm getting better though," Karen said, smiling at Amanda. "Thanks again for talking to us and providing so much information."

"Happy to do it. I'm glad you called, and I hope we can meet sometime. I'll mail that letter today."

"Thank you," Jim said. "We very much appreciate it, and we'll keep you in the loop."

"Good-bye," Phillip said.

Jim disconnected the call. "Well, that was interesting."

"It most certainly was," Karen agreed. "I'll update our genealogy information to say that according to family history, Margarethe was pushed into a river by Albert Kleiner, and Sophia was killed by her husband, Thomas Johnson."

"Thanks. The folder is on the desk in the office," Jim said.

"I think you've just paved the way for a successful search," Amanda observed. "Phillip provided some good insight into your family history, as well as useful information."

"That letter is most disturbing though," Karen said, frowning.

Jim nodded. "Yes, it is. I don't know where this will lead us at this point. We can continue to research what happened to Margarethe, but if she was murdered and her body wasn't found, then we won't find out much."

"I wish there was a way to verify what happened to her. We might have to accept that we'll never know the whole story," Amanda said.

"I agree," Karen said, yawning. "Right now, I feel the need for a nap after that call with Phillip. It's a lot to think about."

"We'll leave in a bit," Jim said, and then turned to Amanda. "Can I trouble you for a drink?"

Amanda wasn't sure if he meant alcohol or water. "I think we all need a drink, but since you have to drive home, you'd better have water," she joked, leading them into the kitchen.

Jim winked as he poured himself a glass of water. "We can do that another time—I hope."

Amanda's heart skipped a beat, but she tried to appear calm on the outside. Inside, though, she was ecstatic. "That sounds nice," she said, and then changed the subject. "We should meet again after you've had time to gather your thoughts on the conversation with Phillip."

"Today is Friday, so let's take a couple of days to do more research," Karen suggested. "We can meet on Monday at noon again if you're available."

"I'm free," Amanda confirmed. "I'll make sandwiches for us, so don't eat lunch before you come." She was happy that Karen was becoming more assertive and comfortable in voicing her opinion.

"Perfect," Jim said.

Chapter 7

After Jim and Karen left, Amanda took Bandy outside and stood on the deck to get some fresh air. She noticed the trees were now totally bare and bristly—their once beautiful leaves were scattered below them. Winter was coming soon. She looked up at the gray sky with mournful eyes, dreading the dreary months ahead in the Midwest.

On top of that, Thanksgiving was approaching, and Amanda always felt sad during the holidays. She'd felt that way even before her grandparents died, because long before that, her parents had died. Amanda didn't remember much about them. She was only three years old when they were killed in a helicopter crash during a sightseeing trip in Hawaii. Her grandparents didn't talk about it much in front of her, although she often saw the sadness in their eyes. She also sensed that they felt lucky to have her with them, but she knew there was a void that would never be filled. That void for Amanda became deeper when her grandparents died. Although her demanding job helped to keep her mind occupied, the loss often became unbearable whenever she was alone. She'd then go back to the office to do paperwork, so she could avoid her own thoughts. As time went on, it became harder to escape—especially when burnout creeped in, and she knew she could no longer continue the job. It was at that point that she began to think about her life before she became a social worker, and she realized she missed her hometown. She was relieved to have been able to buy her grandparents' house. She should never have sold it in the first place.

Amanda continued standing on the deck, her thoughts moving on to Jim. He was the best guy she'd known in a very long time—if not the best she'd ever met. She was no longer afraid to have feelings for him. It seemed wonderfully natural to have him around. A sudden chilly wind made her shiver, so she called for Bandy to come inside. She then decided to call Carolyn. *Perhaps it was time to tell her old friend about Jim*, she thought.

"Well, hello, Amanda," Carolyn answered.

"Hi, there. I thought I'd check in to see how everything is going."

"Everything is fine. Just busy with the kids and husband. I'm in desperate need of a night out. We should do that sometime."

"That sounds fun."

"Let's do it after the holidays," Carolyn said, and then quickly changed the subject. "Anything juicy going on that I need to know about?"

"Why do you ask?" Amanda responded. She wondered if Carolyn had driven by her house when Jim and Karen were there.

"Just a feeling," Carolyn said playfully.

Amanda laughed. "Okay. You caught me. I'll confess."

"And?"

"So, I've met someone I'm falling for rather quickly."

"I knew it! I must say that I'm thrilled for you. This is great news, Amanda! Do you think he feels the same way?"

"I'm getting vibes that he does, but I'm going to be patient on this."

"Well, I hope it moves along quickly. You deserve to be happy, my friend. All the best to you on this."

"Thanks."

"And I'm glad you called to tell me about it."

"Please keep it between you and me. I don't want it getting around town."

"It's our secret—just like old times. We did have our share of secrets, didn't we?"

"Yes, we did!"

"But I'll never tell," Carolyn joked.

Amanda laughed. "The water tower prank was the funniest. Remember when we made a dummy for Halloween and hoisted it up there?"

"How could I ever forget that. One of our best, ever."

"And remember the bottle rocket wars we organized by the river?"

"Boy, we'd never get away with that now. They've cracked down on fireworks these days," Carolyn said, laughing.

Amanda sighed. "I guess we need to do fun grown-up things now. Is there such a thing?"

"Well, if there is, then we'll think of something. I'm sure of that. Hey, I hear one of my kids crying. I'd better go."

"Sure. We'll talk later. Good-bye!"

"Bye!"

Amanda smiled as she clicked off her phone. She had so many great memories of her teenage years with Carolyn. She heated up a frozen dinner in the microwave, and then turned on the television to watch the news. She was just about to take her first bite when her phone buzzed. It was Jim, and he sounded stressed.

"Hello, Amanda. Something strange has happened!"

"What?"

"I received a message on my phone from a man warning us to stop searching for information on the Mueller family. He said there would be consequences if we pursued the matter any further. He didn't leave a name, and when I tried to return the call to the number that appeared on caller ID—it was not in service."

Amanda was stunned. "Wow! That is rather unnerving. I wonder how he got your number and why he's threatening you. Have you told Karen?"

"Yes, and she's quite upset. I probably shouldn't have said anything, but it was just such a surprise to receive a message like that."

"Do you know of anyone who might have called? Anyone at all?"

"No one. I'm absolutely baffled. I don't know what to think."

"I think you should call Phillip and tell him about it. Ask him if he told anyone about your research."

"That's a good idea. What about the man at the cemetery?" Jim asked

"Hank? I doubt he'd know anything, but we can go back there and talk to him on Monday when you come over if you'd like."

"I think we should do that. I'm not going to let this deter our search, but I'm a bit taken aback by the message."

"I agree. It is disturbing. You should report it to the police if you receive another call."

"The police? I don't want to waste their time. It could be nothing."

"Better safe than sorry."

"It depends on whether the caller is threatening our lives."

"Okay. But promise me you'll report it if they do."

"I promise. As far as today goes, I'll call Phillip to see what he says," Jim assured.

"Sounds like the best plan for now, and then we'll go see Hank at the cemetery on Monday," Amanda said. "Hey, did you receive your DNA tests yet?"

"Yes. We got them today. Karen and I will follow the instructions and then send the kits back to the lab."

"I don't know if it will help with this mystery, but you might be able to connect with other relatives."

"That should be interesting, but there might be some I don't want to connect with," Jim said, laughing.

Amanda was glad he had lightened up, but she understood why he'd been so disturbed over the mysterious message he received. "I get it," she said.

Jim paused for a second and then said, "I was serious about having a drink with you. I feel like we've clicked."

"I'd like that," Amanda said without hesitation.

"Karen and I are so glad you came into our lives."

Amanda's heart was racing. "And I am, too."

"Okay, then. It's settled. Let's get this mystery solved, and then we'll plan a night out for the two of us to celebrate."

"That sounds wonderful."

"I'd better call Phillip now."

"You're welcome to call me after you talk to him."

"I'll do that."

"Talk to you later," Amanda said, clicking off her phone. She felt happy and nervous at the same time. She realized she hadn't eaten her microwaved dinner yet, so she quickly devoured it. Bandy begged for scraps, but she was too hungry to share. She decided to go to her computer to do more research on Jim and Karen's family. Perhaps there was a record of Margarethe's death somewhere. However, the phone call Jim received was so disturbing that Amanda had a hard time focusing. She couldn't shake the feeling that the call was a real threat, and her intuition was usually correct. She decided to hold off doing further research for the night.

Jim called back an hour later. "Hi, again," he said. "I spoke to Phillip, and he was just as surprised as we were about the call. I don't know what to think at this point. I guess I'll wait and see if it happens again. Phillip also said he mailed us the copy of the letter that Hans wrote to the preacher."

"This situation is very odd," Amanda said. "Maybe we'll find out something at the cemetery on Monday. If that triggers another call, then we'll know that Hank is talking to someone."

"That sounds like the best thing to do at this point."

"How's Karen doing?"

"She's still upset over this, but I've seen her much worse."

"She might have nightmares tonight."

"I'm counting on it. They seem to come when she's the most anxious."

"Thanks for letting me know about Phillip."

"No problem. I'll see you on Monday."

After they got off the phone, Amanda noticed Bandy was begging to go outside. She let her out and watched from the back door. There were coyotes around the area, and they were known to attack dogs. Bandy quickly did her business and came inside. It was getting late, so Amanda got ready for bed. She had so many things going through her mind, though, so she knew she wouldn't sleep well.

It was indeed a night of fitful sleep, and Amanda awoke the next morning with sore muscles and a dull headache. She remembered that her mind had been filled with a stream of bad visions throughout her dream cycle, including a nightmare about a woman being pushed off a cliff. This, she assumed, was because she had been thinking about Margarethe. She hoped Karen had slept peacefully, but she knew it was probable that it was a bad night for her as well.

Although Amanda was tired, she went to the computer to continue her research. Again, she tried to find out something about Margarethe's death. Unfortunately, there was no obituary, nor were there any newspaper articles about a woman falling to her death in a river. She decided to look up the newspaper clippings about how Margarethe was beaten and left for dead by her former husband, Karl Brinkmann. She'd read them too quickly when she found them before, so she wondered if there might be something she missed. The articles provided the details of the beating, as well as information about the trial. Amanda was amazed at the courage Margarethe must have had to enter the courtroom to testify. It was a cut and dry case. Karl had even confessed to the jail guard that he had attempted to kill her.

As she explored further, she found the article that verified what Jim and Karen had said about Karl being released from prison early. It was written by Albert Kleiner and described how community members were stunned about the attempted murder. He asked everyone to write letters to let the governor know that Karl was an upstanding man and deserved clemency. Even more appalling, though, was that the letter-writing campaign to the governor had worked. Amanda remembered what Phillip had said about Albert pushing Margarethe into the river. She

decided to do a search on the name, *Albert Kleiner*, to
see if there was more information on him. She then
found four men with the same name. Since Margarethe
was beaten in 1870 and two of the men were born after
that year, she narrowed it down to the other two. One
was born in Ohio in 1828; the other was born in 1840,
and he was a German immigrant. He arrived in Illinois
in 1861. Amanda clicked on the Kleiner man who
immigrated to Illinois and found that a detailed family
tree was listed. The tree included people living in the
present day, and she was surprised that one of those
people was Senator Bart Kleiner of Kansas.

Amanda was familiar with Senator Kleiner. She'd
seen his ads during election season which touted his
old-fashioned family values. Like other candidates, he
presented himself as a saint. He was often
photographed while walking through a wheat field and
talking to farmers. Sometimes his beautiful wife and
three young daughters were also featured—all smiling
with brilliant white teeth and perfectly coiffed hair.
However, Amanda had heard rumors about the man
contrary to how he presented himself. The rumors
ranged from illicit affairs on his wife, campaign fraud,
and even speculations that he had people killed who got
in his way. There were certainly a few who had crossed
Kleiner, and they were later found dead. However, it
was always ruled that the deaths were due to some sort
of an accident. Of course, the rumors might not be true,
and it was certainly possible they were sparked by an
enemy. The campaign fraud charge had gone to court,
but the senator was found to be innocent. As for the
illicit affairs—no one had come forward to formally
accuse Kleiner yet—maybe out of fear—or perhaps the
stories were rumors after all. The voters never really
knew for sure. Yes, politics were a slimy business. One
needed to question everything being reported these

days, especially stories shared on social media, which was one of the reasons Amanda stayed away from online social networking. She had no desire to read stuff like that. However, there was one thing for certain. Each one of the local media outlets reported that Senator Bart Kleiner was planning to run for President of the United States in the upcoming election.

Amanda then searched for any newspaper articles from the late 1800s which might mention that Albert Kleiner was suspected of Margarethe's disappearance. She found nothing relating to him in that regard. Since Albert seemed to have had power and had led the effort to get Margarethe's husband out of prison, perhaps the community protected him.

Amanda decided to wait until Monday to tell Jim and Karen about Senator Kleiner being a descendant of Albert. She knew there was no proof that the senator made the threatening call to Jim, but she had a feeling it was so. She was not one to believe in conspiracy theories and hated the vile slander, but sometimes there was truth to a story.

The next morning, Amanda stopped by Carolyn's house to drink coffee and chat, but she didn't stay long. Of course, Carolyn was curious about the budding romance she had mentioned on the phone. She told her that things were progressing slowly, but there was indeed something brewing. Carolyn grinned and gave a "thumbs up," and Amanda promised to keep her updated on the progress. She felt like a high school girl again—like a teenager gossiping about boys. Before she walked out the door, she turned and hugged her friend and pledged to get together again soon. She decided to go home and pick up Bandy to go for a drive, who was quite excited at the prospect of getting out of the house.

Amanda drove slowly on the gravel roads outside of town to avoid chipping the paint on her car. She turned on her headlights because of the cloudy, misty conditions, which was typical for a November day in Kansas. The weather was another reminder that Thanksgiving was approaching quickly, and she had no idea what she was going to do that day.

Chapter 8

Amanda awoke on Monday morning feeling excited for the next adventure with Jim and Karen. As usual, she brewed coffee, took care of Bandy, and then got ready for the day. She decided to be a bit more adventurous in her style by wearing a leopard-print sweater and jeans. Her shoes were casual flats that matched the print on the sweater.

Amanda remembered she'd promised to make sandwiches for the meeting, so she was glad she had sliced meat, cheese, lettuce, and pickles in the refrigerator. She laid everything out on a platter, along with baby carrots and celery. She then set the table with plates, napkins, and glasses for water. Although it looked like a summer picnic, the weather outside was dreary and cold, so she retrieved a heavy jacket from the closet for the trip to the cemetery.

When Jim and Karen arrived, Amanda met them at the door before they rang the bell. Karen looked as if she'd had no sleep, and she was visibly shaken by the small twitch in her hands. Amanda asked how she was doing on the way to the kitchen. Jim frowned as they walked.

"I had nightmares all night," Karen replied.

"I'm sorry they're continuing," Amanda said. She then decided to change the subject to lighten the mood. "Do you feel like eating?"

"Sure," Karen answered.

Amanda remembered she needed to set out mustard and mayonnaise, so she took the jars from the refrigerator and placed them on the table along with a pitcher of water. "Do you want anything else to drink? I can make coffee if you'd like."

"I just want water," Karen said.

Jim smiled. "Yes, that's fine with me, too."

Bandy sat near the table begging for scraps, bobbing back and forth like a baseball player waiting to catch a fly ball.

"Do you mind if I give her something?" Jim asked. "She acts like she's starving, but I know better than that. I'm sure she is very spoiled."

Amanda nodded. "Yes, she can have a carrot."

Jim dropped the carrot, and Bandy devoured it instantly. The begging continued.

"All gone!" Amanda declared, putting up her hands to show they were empty.

Jim turned to her. "Karen and I were wondering if you have plans for Thanksgiving. We'd love to have you spend it with us."

Amanda was a bit surprised by the invitation, but she was thrilled. "That would be great! Thank you for asking."

Karen smiled for the first time since arriving. "I'm happy we'll be together. We can work out the details later."

"Absolutely," Amanda said.

Jim grinned. "Well, good. We were afraid you might have other plans."

They finished their sandwiches and put the plates and glasses in the dishwasher before going into the office. Amanda knew it was time to tell them about the Kleiner family information she'd found. After they were seated, she asked, "Did you receive any other strange calls this weekend?"

Jim shook his head. "No, and we didn't do any research either. That phone call was so disturbing that I needed a break."

Karen nodded.

"I did some research on my own, and I discovered some interesting information about the Kleiner family."

Jim raised his eyebrows. "I can't wait to hear it."

"I began with a search on Albert Kleiner—the man mentioned in Hans's letter that he sent to the preacher—the man who allegedly pushed Margarethe into the river. I couldn't find any newspaper clippings about her death, nor any articles suggesting he pushed her over a cliff. What I did find was the family tree of Albert Kleiner, which included a list of descendants who are still living. Senator Bart Kleiner is one of them."

"I know who he is," Karen said slowly. He's known to be a womanizer and a jerk."

"That's what I've heard, too," Jim agreed.

"Did you also know that he plans to run for president?" Amanda asked.

"Yes, and he has a good chance of winning, unfortunately," Jim responded.

Karen's eyes narrowed. "I hope not."

"You might also have heard rumors about people who have crossed Senator Kleiner and ended up dead. There's never been proof of foul play though," Amanda continued.

Jim nodded. "I've heard those rumors as well."

"That's disturbing," Karen said. "I never know what to believe anymore though."

"I just thought I'd let you know what I've found. It could be nothing or it could be something that leads us to answers."

"Exactly," Jim agreed. "Let's go to the cemetery and ask Hank some questions."

"I'm ready," Karen said, standing and stretching.

"Okay. I'll let the dog out and then meet you at the car," Amanda said.

She got up and escorted the Dorions to the front door. Bandy ran to the back door, as if she knew she'd better go quickly, and fortunately, she did. Amanda then grabbed her coat and went outside to the driveway, where Jim and Karen were waiting by the car. She was going to get in the back seat, but Karen motioned for her to sit in the front.

Jim smiled, and Amanda got the impression they had discussed the seating arrangement while they were waiting. She was pleased, however, to be closer to him.

The same white Honda Civic was parked at the cemetery, which meant Hank was probably inside the business office. Amanda took a deep breath as she got out of the car. She hoped he'd know why Jim received the phone call.

The door was unlocked, so they walked inside to find Hank standing behind the counter looking at his computer screen. He jumped and took off his reading glasses when he realized Amanda, Karen, and Jim were there.

"I'm sorry. We didn't mean to startle you," Amanda said gently.

"That's quite all right. I was just deep in thought," Hank responded, frowning.

Amanda thought he seemed rather nervous, but she decided not to ask about it.

Jim got straight to the point. "We're here to ask you a question, and I hope you can help us with that."

"I don't know anything, I swear. I'm just a volunteer here!"

Hank was certainly defensive, Amanda thought. She and Karen exchanged uncomfortable glances, and Jim continued.

"Hold on. We're not here to blame you for anything or interrogate you. Why are you so upset?"

"I don't want any trouble."

"There is no trouble. We're just confused about something. That's all."

"Confused about w-what?" Hank stammered. He moved his right hand to his left shoulder and began to nervously rub it, as if his muscles were tight from stress.

"I received a phone message from a man warning me to stop researching the Mueller family. He didn't provide his name, and his number was out of service when I tried to return the call. Did you tell anyone we were here asking about the family?"

Hank's face went pale, and he began to sweat. Amanda was worried the man was going to have a heart attack. "Are you okay?" she asked.

"I'm fine."

"Just in case, perhaps we should take you to the hospital," Amanda offered.

"No. That won't be necessary. I just need to sit down and drink a glass of water. I've had the flu recently, and I'm afraid I'm still a bit weak and dehydrated."

Amanda pointed at a refrigerator in the back of the room. "Do you have any bottled water in there?"

"Yes. I can get it though."

"No. Please sit down. I'll get it," Amanda said, quickly approaching the refrigerator. It was loaded with bottles of water and soda. "Would you rather have soda?"

"Just water," Hank answered. He was sitting down and seemed to be doing better. Amanda handed the bottle to him.

Jim moved closer to Hank and spoke softly. "I'm sorry. I didn't mean to upset you. We're just trying to solve a mystery in our family, and we found it odd that I would receive such a phone call."

Hank glanced at Karen, and she nodded in agreement.

Amanda remained quiet and let Jim do the talking. She was impressed with his gentleness toward the man.

Hank took a few sips of water before speaking. "I'll answer your question, but you must not repeat what I have to say."

"You have our word," Jim assured.

"We won't tell anyone," Karen promised.

Hank looked at Amanda. "You can trust us completely," she said.

"Well, then. After you left the other day, I noticed something else written on the database file for Sophia Mueller Johnson," Hank explained. "There was a notation with instructions to call a phone number and enter code *1882* should anyone ever inquire about her. I made the call, not knowing why I was supposed to do it. After two rings, an automated voice said to enter the code. I entered *1882* and realized that it was the year Sophia was born. A few seconds later, a man answered and wanted to verify that the code was for Sophia. I acknowledged it was the right name and matched the number in the cemetery database. The man then asked if anyone had requested information about the woman. I told him that three people had come into the office asking about her. He asked for names, but I said that I could only remember the names *Jim and Karen*—family members of Sophia. He wasn't interested in Amanda anyway since she's not related. He wanted to know if questions were asked about any other people with the Mueller name. I told him that you originally came to find out about Margarethe and Hans, but I had no information on them. The man said to call him again if you ever returned here and asked about the Mueller family. I requested his name, and he refused to provide it. He then said to never tell you about the phone call, or I wouldn't like the consequences. I don't know what he meant by that, but I didn't like it. It sounded like a threat."

Karen gasped. Amanda sighed, and Jim did a slow whistle. None of this helped Hank's nerves. He began rubbing his shoulder again, and his hands were trembling.

"Are you sure you don't want us to take you to the hospital?" Amanda asked.

"No. I'm fine."

Jim stood up. "It's interesting that the man used the word *consequences* in both phone calls," he said.

"I just thought of something," Amanda said. "Maybe we should check the database to see if all of the Mueller family members have a phone number and code listed by their names."

"That would be interesting to find out," Karen said.

"I can check for you," Hank offered.

"Are you feeling better?" Amanda asked.

"I'm okay," Hank responded, getting up to go to the computer. He logged in and typed the surname. He gasped as his eyes widened.

"What is it?" Jim asked.

"I've never noticed this on any surname I've checked in the past, but beside each Mueller name, it says to discreetly call a phone number and enter a code. Each phone number is different. Sophia's code was the year she was born. I'll check to see if that is the case on each name listed."

Jim, Karen, and Amanda waited patiently while he looked up the files.

"Can we read them, too?" Karen asked.

"I don't see why not. You can stand behind me."

As they peered over his shoulder, Hank asked if there was a specific name they wanted to see.

"Johann Mueller," Jim answered quickly. "He was our great-grandfather, and he was born in 1879."

Hank scrolled to the name. "Well, I'll be," he said. "The code is indeed *1879*, so this appears to be the pattern. I'll check the others." He continued to click on names and found that each code matched the birth year.

"The question is, are you going to call any of the phone numbers after we leave to report that we asked about the people?" Jim inquired.

"I won't call again. There's something not right about this, and I don't understand why anyone would need to know if someone comes here to ask about their relatives. I should never have called the first time. I did feel threatened, but I didn't think I should go to the police about it. There's nothing they can do at this point. The thing that gets me is that I know the phone numbers are probably untraceable. I have a suspicion this person has the power to do that."

"Or maybe they're using burner phones," Amanda offered.

"But then someone would have to input new phone numbers on the database if the phones are tossed," Jim said.

"Maybe they have the power to obtain the same number again if needed," Karen offered.

Amanda sighed. "Not sure if they can do that, but they must have some sort of system."

Jim's eyes narrowed as he tapped his forefinger on his lips. "Let's try some other surnames to see if there are phone numbers and codes."

"I'll check," Hank said. "But remember, I've never noticed this before. I'd also like to know how these codes got into the database in the first place." He began with the surnames starting with the letter, *A*. There were a lot of names, but the computer was quick. No instructions were written on the files. "It will take more time to go through the alphabet and look at each name, but I'll do it if you want," Hank offered.

"That's okay. You don't have to do that. I was just curious," Jim said.

"I might do it in my spare time. I get rather bored unless another volunteer is here with me."

"I thought you were the only volunteer. Do you think someone else might know about how the codes were received into the system?" Jim asked.

"There are a couple of volunteers who come in now and then but not very often. Sometimes they're here alone and sometimes I'm with them. It's not uncommon for people to call the office with information on their families, so we type it into the database. One of the other volunteers probably input the codes next to the Mueller names, due to someone calling the office. I probably wasn't here that day."

"Did you tell anyone about the call you received?" Amanda asked.

"I told my friend, Debbie Blake, but she would never repeat it. We're kind of an item, you see," Hank said, snickering.

"I guess there's nothing we can do right now," Jim said. "If no one calls the number, the man will never know we've been here. We probably won't hear from him again."

"Thanks so much for your time, Hank," Karen said.

Jim smiled and extended his hand. "Yes, thank you. We appreciate it." He then pulled his wallet from his pocket and took out his business card. "Here's my card. If you hear anything about why there is such an interest in the Mueller family, please don't hesitate to call me."

Hank took the card. "I'll do that. It's been nice meeting you folks."

"Likewise," Amanda said. She had tried to keep as quiet as possible during the visit, because she thought it was best for Jim and Karen to take the lead. This was about their family after all.

Dark clouds filled the sky when they walked back to the car. Karen smiled at Amanda and then climbed into the back seat, indicating the seating arrangement was the same for the return trip. As Jim's car inched along on the gravel, Amanda noticed a fancy dark-blue sedan parked on the side of the road. She couldn't tell if anyone was inside though, because the windows were tinted.

Jim nodded toward the car. "I thought it was illegal to have such dark tint on the windows."

"I did, too," Amanda said.

"So, what do you think about what Hank told us?" Karen asked.

Amanda responded first. "I think it's creepy."

"I agree," Jim said. "I don't know what we can do about it though. I'll call Phillip to let him know what we found out."

"Let's talk about Thanksgiving," Karen said, changing the subject.

"Good idea," Jim said. "Should we have it at our house? Amanda's never been there."

"That sounds great," Karen agreed.

"I'd like that," Amanda said quietly, yet firmly. She was trying to seem calm about the invitation, because she didn't want to come across as a lonely person eager for companionship on the holiday. However, she also wanted the Dorions to know she was appreciative of their hospitality.

"Okay, well, you know it's the next Thursday after this one, right?" Jim said.

"I do. What would you like for me to bring?"

"What's your specialty?"

"I don't really have one. I hate to admit it, but I'm not a great cook," Amanda said. "I do have my grandma's green bean casserole recipe, which was quite delicious when she made it."

Jim grinned. "That sounds good. Bring the ingredients, and we can cook the dinner together. You should probably be at our place by nine o'clock in the morning. I'll text you with the address."

"I'll plan on it. Thanks again for inviting me."

"We're happy to have you," Karen said.

"Ditto that," Jim agreed.

Chapter 9

They chatted about happy things the rest of the way to Amanda's house—about childhood summer camp, riding bikes, climbing trees, and family trips. Amanda was thankful she'd had the good sense to return Jim's desperate call about Karen in the not-so-distant past. She shuddered to think she might never have met them.

After they arrived, Jim walked her to the door. "When should we meet again?" he asked.

"Let's meet on Friday and keep the time at noon if you're free."

"My schedule is flexible, so high noon, it is. I've noticed such a change in Karen since we've met, so even if I have a work meeting, I'll clear the time. I'd do anything to make sure she continues to get better. I'd also like to see you myself."

Amanda felt her face get warm, and she knew she was blushing. "Thank you. That means a lot to me."

"I'll see you Friday," he said, shaking her hand, and then turned to leave.

Amanda felt the warmth of her face extend throughout her body. She kept her composure and called after him. "I'll look forward to that."

Karen had moved to the front seat of the car, and she was smiling and waving. Amanda returned the gesture. She watched the Dorions pull out of the driveway before going inside, where Bandy was barking excitedly. She felt a bit guilty for leaving her for so long but remembered that the dog was alone much longer when she worked full time. She reached down and stroked her head, and Bandy sniffed incessantly, probably smelling the residue of Jim's cologne from their handshake. Amanda could smell it, too. There was just a hint of spice, which reminded her of the cologne her grandfather used. She let Bandy outside, but the hungry hound was soon at the door begging to come inside. She poured some kibble and leftover meat into the feeding bowl and watched as she gobbled it up. She then decided to take a nap.

When Amanda woke up, she made a grilled cheese sandwich and sat down in her black leather chair which was positioned in front of the television. She scrolled through the channels with her remote until she found her favorite local news show. It was five o'clock, so the most important stories of the day were being shown. The first reports were about several robberies in the Kansas City area. Amanda took a bite of her sandwich and was in the process of chewing, when the news anchor announced that an elderly man had been attacked at a cemetery in Hillsdale. She gasped and nearly choked on her food. She waited breathlessly for the details, hoping it wasn't Hank Autin, but his photo and name soon appeared on the screen. Hank had survived the attack, but he was in the hospital. She grabbed her phone to dial Jim, but it rang before she could complete the call. She answered. It was Jim, and he sounded breathless.

"Amanda, someone has been in our house! They rummaged through my room and sliced up my pillows, comforter, and sheets. They also vandalized Karen's bedroom—went through her drawers and sliced through her bedding. My office has also been ransacked. The drawers from my desk were yanked out, and papers are strewn across the floor. A folder where I kept genealogy information is missing. They even smashed my computer."

Amanda was so stunned that her voice was shaky and high-pitched when she spoke. "Did you call the police?"

"Yes. I filed a report, and two officers came over and inspected the damage. They wanted to know if Karen and I have any enemies. We don't have any that I know of, but now I'm starting to wonder about that phone call I received. I told the police about it. They admitted it might be connected to what happened here today!"

"This is unbelievable! How is Karen?"

"She's standing next to me right now, and she's very shaken up. I hate to ask this, but would it be okay if she stays the night with you?"

"Absolutely. Do you want to stay, too?"

"I think I'll stay here to watch the place tonight, but thanks for the offer."

Amanda could no longer hold in the news about Hank. "Well, I don't want to alarm you any further, but you might want to plan on spending the evening at my place, even if you don't stay all night. I have just seen on the news that Hank Autin was severely beaten at the cemetery. He's in the hospital, and I'm assuming it's the one in Paola. I'm going to go see him, and I think we need to talk to the police."

Jim was silent, and Amanda knew he was trying to process the information. When he spoke, his voice was nearly a whisper. "We'll be there as soon as we can, and we'll both stay as long as necessary. I'd better go ahead and spend the night at your house, because I'm worried you might also be in danger. I'll send Phillip a message to let him know what happened—just in case he needs to be warned. We'll get packed up and be there within the hour, and then we'll go see Hank and talk to the police. Take care until then."

"See you soon," Amanda said before ending the connection. She then checked the spare bedrooms and bathrooms to make sure they were presentable for guests. The only things needed were towels, wash cloths, and soap. She was glad she kept a stock of extra toiletries just in case she needed them. Bandy followed her around the house and began barking with excitement. Amanda knew she probably sensed the stress in the air.

Even though she rarely used the home alarm system, she decided it was a good idea to set it until Jim and Karen arrived. She called the hospital in Paola to make sure Hank had been taken there. Patient Information confirmed he was there and currently in stable condition. Amanda was relieved to hear that. She went into the office, then sat exhaustedly in one of the wingback chairs and waited impatiently for Jim and Karen. Her phone vibrated in her hand, and she quickly looked at the screen. It was a text from Karen to let her know they were almost there. She let Bandy outside for a bit and then locked up again. The alarm system beeped with every door she opened, but there weren't any motion sensors inside the house.

Amanda stood at the front window and watched for Jim and Karen to pull into the driveway. Time seemed to be at a standstill, and she wondered how it had come to be that she was in the middle of such a strange situation. After all, she had come back home to get away from stress, and now she was feeling rather anxious. But in this case, although her adrenaline was pumping, Amanda felt alive and hopeful. She knew that meeting Jim and helping Karen, along with the anticipation of solving the mystery of Margarethe had a lot to do with that. She was also hopeful for a happily-ever-after story. Of course, she knew that no one truly lives in a fairy tale sort of world. Still, she knew that if she found someone with whom to share her life, she wouldn't feel so alone in the world. Perhaps Jim was the man who would fill that void. She realized that just a few weeks ago, she'd been perfectly content to lead a quiet life without work meetings or complications. However, getting to know Jim and Karen had changed that notion, and she now looked forward to activity. Her thoughts were interrupted as she heard a car pulling into the gravel driveway. Bandy barked and ran to the door, and Amanda looked outside to make sure it was indeed Jim and Karen who had arrived. She breathed a sigh of relief when she saw their car, and then turned off the alarm system.

"I'm so glad you're both okay and no one was in your house when you arrived," Amanda said as she opened the front door. She noticed Karen was very pale.

"It was a shock to come home to that," Jim said, shaking his head.

Amanda put her hand on Karen's shoulder. "Would you like a drink of water before we leave?"

"That would be great."

Jim nodded. "I'll take one, too."

They went into the kitchen, and Amanda pulled three glasses from the cabinet so they could each make their drinks. She noticed that Karen's hands were shaking as she held her glass against the icemaker lever. "We're going to get through this together," Amanda assured.

Karen didn't seem too convinced. There were tears in her eyes. "I was feeling so much better, and now I'm back to where I started. My nerves are shot."

Jim frowned and faced his sister. "Everything is going to be okay. I'm going to find out who is behind this."

Karen nodded slowly. "I'm sorry I'm like this."

"Don't ever apologize for being yourself. You're a wonderful person who is dealing with a great amount of stress," Amanda said.

"Thank you."

Jim changed the subject. "Do you know anything about Hank yet?"

"He's in the hospital in stable condition. That's all they would tell me on the phone."

"I can't believe this has happened. I hope our visit isn't what prompted the beating."

Amanda shook her head. "We can't blame ourselves. We had no way of knowing this would happen."

"We should go there now to check on him, don't you think?" Karen said grimly.

Amanda nodded. "Yes. Let's head over there now. I can drive."

"That would probably be best, because no one would recognize your car—just in case we're being watched," Jim said.

"Agreed." Amanda motioned for them to follow her through the kitchen. "My car is on the other side of the garage, so just leave yours where it is. You can exit first, because I need to set the alarm system. We don't need to come home to any surprises."

"Good idea to set it," Jim said, as he pressed the button to open the garage door.

"I also have a bark alarm that serves as a deterrent," Amanda said, pointing at Bandy.

Jim smiled and nodded.

After ensuring the alarm was on and working properly, Amanda got behind the wheel of her car and backed out of the garage. She pressed a button on her remote, and then waited until the door closed completely before pulling out of the driveway. Jim was sitting in the front passenger seat, and Karen was in the back.

"Nice car," Jim observed. "I didn't peg you as a Volvo driver though."

"Its name is *Mister Turtle!* And what kind of car did you *peg* me as owning?"

"Based on your personality, I thought you'd be driving a little red sports car."

"Seriously? Why would you think that? I'm not the flashy type!"

"I hope you know I'm joking. There's no way I could have guessed, but I think *Mister Turtle* fits as well," Jim said, winking.

Amanda grinned back at him. She was embarrassed she'd taken the comment seriously, because he was obviously trying to lighten the mood.

The drive to the hospital was only ten miles, and they arrived in short order. Amanda backed into a space and looked around the parking lot to make sure no one was watching. They walked quickly inside to the lobby. There was a young woman talking on the phone at the front desk. She smiled and held up her forefinger to indicate they should wait until she was done. They stood nearby and waited. It wasn't long before the woman motioned for them to come back to the desk.

"Sorry about that," she apologized. "We've had several calls about a patient this evening. How may I help you?"

"We're looking for Hank Autin's room," Jim answered.

"He's in room 122. I have it memorized now, since he's the one people keep calling about," she said, pointing to the right.

"Thanks," Jim said. "Would you happen to know if the police have been here?"

"They were here when Hank was being admitted, but I haven't seen them for a while. I'm just glad he's okay."

"We are, too," Amanda said, and then turned to walk toward the room.

"Thanks again," Jim called as they made their way down the hall.

The door to Hank's room was closed, but male voices were faintly audible in the hall.

"What should we do?" Jim asked. "I hate to interrupt them."

"I think we should knock anyway," Karen said boldly.

Amanda nodded and tilted her head toward the door to indicate they should announce their presence.

Karen tapped lightly on the door, and the voices inside the room were instantly hushed. A few long seconds passed before a police officer opened the door.

"Who are you?" the officer asked.

Amanda noticed the name on his badge said, *Jeremy Crenshaw*. He appeared to be around 45 years of age and had blue eyes, rosy skin, and light brown hair. He was tall and fit, and quite good looking. Amanda introduced herself, and then made the introductions for Jim and Karen. She then said, "I'm sorry to interrupt you. We met Mr. Autin at the cemetery, and we came to check on him."

"Hold on," Officer Crenshaw said, turning his head to the side. "Do you know these people, Hank?"

"Yes. They're okay," he mumbled.

Crenshaw motioned for them to come inside. "I can step outside if you'd like to visit with him alone."

"Actually, we'd like to talk to you, too," Jim said before entering.

Crenshaw raised his eyebrows but displayed no other indication of surprise at the request. "Do you have information about the attack?"

"Not exactly, but something has happened that we feel might be connected to it," Jim answered quickly.

Crenshaw nodded. "Well, then, come on in and have a seat."

As they walked into the room, they each nodded to Hank. He was awake and alert, but his face was barely recognizable. There were bandages covering his nose, which was obviously broken. His eyes were swollen, but his left eye was the worst. It was barely open, and there was already obvious bruising. His lips were also swollen and had been bleeding. His left arm was in a sling.

Amanda said, "We're so sorry this happened to you, Hank."

"We came as soon as we heard," Karen added.

Jim frowned and shook his head. "I don't understand who would do this to you."

"I don't either," Hank whispered.

Crenshaw pointed to three chairs by the window. "Please sit down and tell me what has happened and why you think it might be connected to this."

They pulled the chairs closer to Hank's bed. Crenshaw stood between them, as if he were on guard.

"Okay," Jim said calmly. "I'll start from the beginning."

He looked directly at Officer Crenshaw and told him about how they had been researching their family history and had enlisted Amanda for help. He didn't mention that she'd originally been Karen's therapist.

Amanda was glad about that—not because she thought that seeing a therapist was something to hide—but because it was Karen's personal business, and she was the only one who should discuss it. Karen's body language became more relaxed, indicating that she was relieved as well. Jim explained they'd come to the cemetery to search for family graves but couldn't find two of the names they were seeking. They then went to the office to ask about Hans and Margarethe Mueller. Hank searched the database for the names, but there was no indication they were buried there. In addition, because they had noticed a missing headstone in the family plot, he looked that up, too. He found that Sophia Mueller Johnson was buried there, but no stone was ever placed in her honor.

Crenshaw frowned and crossed his arms. He seemed to be growing impatient. "So, how is any of this connected to Hank's beating?"

"I'm getting to that," Jim responded. "Several days later, I received a message on my phone from a man threatening that I'd better stop researching the Mueller family or there would be consequences. I tried to respond to the call, but the number was out of service."

"Did you tell anyone else about your research?" Crenshaw interrupted.

"Just a relative we never knew about until recently."

"And the name of that individual is?"

"His name is Phillip Mueller. He provided us with some additional information on the family."

"Continue," Crenshaw said sternly.

"Later, after talking to Phillip—that's when I received the phone message warning me to stop searching. After telling my sister and Amanda about the call, I rang Phillip again to see if he'd mentioned our conversation to anyone. He had not. In fact, he was just as puzzled as I was about the strange phone message."

"Do you believe he was telling the truth?"

"Sure. He has no reason to lie about it. He's from the same Mueller line, and he was very honest about our history."

"And what is your history, exactly?"

"Karen and I have a great-great-grandmother who was nearly beaten to death by her husband after she came to the United States. Fortunately, they had no children, and she was granted a divorce. The man was sentenced to prison, but he was released early. Our great-great-grandmother later disappeared after marrying our great-great-grandfather and having several children. Phillip provided information on what might have happened to her, but he also mentioned there had been threats made to our ancestors."

"What kind of threats?" Crenshaw asked, taking a pen and paper from a table. He was now apparently intrigued by the history.

"Death threats," Jim responded.

"Has Phillip been threatened?"

"Not that I know of."

Crenshaw jotted down something on the paper. "Why would he not have been threatened with the same phone call you received? He's from the same line of people."

"I don't know. Perhaps it's because he hasn't been searching for ancestry information and we were."

"Okay. That's fair enough, but it's still odd."

"I agree."

"Again, how might this be tied in with what happened to Hank?"

"We went to see him again today to find out if he'd mentioned our search to anyone. He told us that he found a notation on the database file for our great-great-aunt Sophia. The notation indicated that if anyone were ever to inquire about her, someone from the cemetery was supposed to call a number and then enter a code. Hank made the call and was connected to a man who wanted to know if information had been requested. He told him that three people had come in to ask about the Mueller family. The man asked for our names, but Hank could only remember mine and Karen's. The man said to call again if anyone ever returned to inquire about the family. He also said that if Hank told anyone about the call, he wouldn't like the consequences. I'm sure Hank has mentioned this."

At that point, Hank mumbled the word, "No."

"He's had a hard time speaking," Crenshaw said. "Did anything else happen?"

"Yes, it most certainly did."

"When my sister and I arrived at our home, we found that someone had broken into it. They ransacked the place, but nothing of value was stolen—except my genealogy folder, which included the research on our family."

Crenshaw's eyes widened. "Did you file a police report? I haven't heard anything about this. Where do you live?"

"We live in Overland Park, Kansas—a suburb of Kansas City."

"I know it's a suburb," Crenshaw said, rolling his eyes. "How long ago did you file the report?"

"Not long before we came here. I called Amanda after the officers left, and she told me she'd just seen on the news that Hank had been badly beaten. We came as fast as we could, and we were hoping to talk with the police about what happened to my house, so I'm glad you were here."

"I'm glad I was, too. Hank has been a friend to my family for years, and I plan on staying as long as I can in case the goons come to the hospital to finish the job."

"Goons? So…there was more than one person who attacked him?"

Crenshaw nodded. "Yes. There were two of them."

"Horrible," said Jim. "I don't believe they wanted to kill him though—or they would have done it. I think they wanted to rough him up to keep him quiet. Perhaps it was a warning."

"Might be, but I'm not going to take a risk. Is there anything else?"

Amanda had been quiet long enough. "Yes. There was a dark-blue sedan parked on the side of the road near the cemetery when we left today. We noticed it because the windows were tinted so dark that it was impossible to determine if anyone was in it."

"Sorry. I forgot about that," Jim said.

"That is interesting," Crenshaw responded, writing quickly. "Did you, by chance, get the license number, or can you give me the make and model of the vehicle?"

"It might have been a Cadillac or a Lincoln," Karen answered quickly, "but we didn't get the license number."

Amanda nodded in agreement and Jim shrugged. They weren't entirely sure of the model—just that it was a nice car.

Jim looked at Hank, who appeared to be about ready to go to sleep. "What did your attackers look like?"

"Both of them were large, bald-headed men."

"Did they say anything?" Jim asked.

Hank grimaced in pain as he spoke. "Yes. To keep my mouth shut from now on, and they were going to teach me a lesson, so I'd be sure to do it in the future. Then they started beating me up. I pretended to be knocked out, and I heard one of them say that Simon would be pleased."

Amanda, Jim, and Karen exchanged glances.

Jim started to speak, but Crenshaw interrupted. "He needs to rest. Visiting hours are over anyway."

Karen stood and moved her chair aside, then put her hand on the bed. "I hope you feel better soon."

"We all do," Jim added as he and Amanda began moving their chairs back toward the window.

Officer Crenshaw walked them out to the hall. "Please keep me informed if anything else happens. I've written down the information, and I'll get in touch with the Overland Park Police Department about your report with them as well. What's your contact information?"

Jim provided his address, email, and phone number, and then said, "We'll definitely keep you posted if something else happens."

"These guys need to be caught. I'll do everything in my power to do that, but I need to have more information. They're probably not from this area or Hank would have recognized them."

Jim nodded. "I have a feeling they're from very far away."

"I do, too," Amanda agreed.

"Thanks for your time," Karen said.

Crenshaw's eyes twinkled as he responded to her, and his tone was softer. "Glad to have met you."

Chapter 10

The ride back to the house was filled with lively conversation about what to do next. Amanda thought they should enlist the help of a private investigator, but Jim wasn't sure about that. Karen agreed wholeheartedly though. After a quick discussion, it was settled that a private investigator would be involved. Amanda knew of a good one, because she'd met the guy when she worked at the clinic. There were several private investigators who came in to ask questions about clients. However, none of the counselors at the clinic could provide information due to client confidentiality. There was one, though, that Amanda liked the most. His name was Mike Kennedy, and although he seemed rather quirky, he was very respectful and professional. And as luck would have it, she still had his business card. She decided to tell the Dorions about him later.

Amanda stopped in her driveway so the Dorions could retrieve their overnight bags from Jim's Subaru. As soon as they got out of her car, she opened the garage door and pulled inside to wait for them. They returned shortly, suitcases in tow, so she pressed the button to shut the door. Jim and Karen stood next to her while she opened the door that led to the kitchen and keyed in the alarm code. Bandy barked and ran into the room as if they were intruders. Amanda stroked her head. "Good girl," she said. "You'll scare them away if they come here."

"Does anything look disturbed at all?" Jim asked, looking around.

"Not that I can see, and the alarm system would have gone off if anyone came inside."

"Okay. I'm going to walk around outside to see if there are any signs that someone might have been here. Do you have a flashlight?"

Amanda nodded. "Sure. It's in my utility drawer." She pulled out the flashlight and handed it to Jim. "Why don't you take Bandy with you. That way she can do her business and let you know if anyone's hanging around out there."

Jim opened the back door. "Good idea," he said, snapping his fingers for the dog to follow. She darted out behind him.

"I think I'll stay inside," Karen said. "I'm a little keyed up after everything that's gone on today."

"I am, too," Amanda agreed. "It's been a long day. If you'd like, I'll show you to your room and you can go wind down in there."

Karen picked up her suitcase. "I'd like that."

Amanda led her to the room and showed her the guest bathroom. "You'll find towels in the cabinet below the sink."

"Thanks so much," Karen said as she laid her suitcase on the bed.

"And you know where the kitchen is in case you need to get a glass of water or midnight snack."

"Thanks. I might do that."

Amanda decided she needed a drink—perhaps something a bit stiffer than water. She walked back to the kitchen and poured herself a glass of red wine. The door opened, and Jim walked inside with Bandy close behind him.

"Hitting it hard tonight, are you?" he joked, pointing at the wine bottle on the counter.

"I sure am. Do you want some?"

"That would be great. Thanks."

Amanda filled a glass halfway and handed it to him. "Let's go to the great room where it's more comfortable. You locked the back door, right?"

"Yes, it's locked," Jim replied as they walked. He looked around the room and then asked, "Where's Karen?"

"She was feeling stressed, so she went to her room to relax."

"That's probably for the best. I just hope she doesn't have any nightmares tonight."

They sat down on the couch together and propped their feet up on the large circular ottoman. Amanda decided to bring up the topic of the private investigator. "I know you have reservations about hiring a PI, but I think it would help in finding out who's threatening you."

Jim frowned as he swallowed a sip of wine. "I get it, but it's just not something I'd ever thought I'd have to do. It also seems like such an infringement of privacy."

"But your privacy has already been compromised. Remember, someone broke into your house."

He sighed. "I know. Full confession here—I had a hard time sending in the DNA sample, too."

"I'm sorry. I had no idea that would bother you. I've done it, and I found it to be a benign thing. It told me about my ancestry, and then I was able to contact people I matched. I've met relatives I never knew I had, and we're now friends."

"That sounds interesting."

"Do you have any aunts, uncles, or cousins?" Amanda asked.

"I have an aunt and a cousin from my father's side of the family, but they live in Alaska. We weren't a close family. Karen is really all I have as far as a blood relative."

"I'll bet you'll find others after your DNA test results arrive. Honestly, it isn't a big deal," Amanda assured, looking into his eyes. She noticed for the first time that there were dark circles under them, making him appear to be very tired.

"Let's talk about you," Jim said, obviously trying to deflect the conversation away from his family.

"I'm just a person who got burned out from a demanding job in the city, so I came running home."

"I have to say that this is a very nice place to call your home, and I think you made a wise decision. I love the peacefulness I feel here—or maybe it's you that makes me feel that way," Jim said, leaning closer. Amanda thought he was going to kiss her, but he didn't, which made her feel rather disappointed.

"Thank you. It's just what I needed. I only wish my grandparents were alive."

"Were you close to your parents?"

"They were killed in a helicopter crash when I was only three years old. Sadly, I don't remember much about them. I remember thinking my mother looked like a fairy tale princess though, and she used to read to me a lot."

"I'm sorry to hear that," Jim said, shaking his head. "It is a sad irony that both of us lost our parents in traumatic events."

"It certainly is, at that," Amanda said, and then noticing Jim's glass was empty, she asked, "Would you like another glass of wine?"

"No thanks. I'm good," Jim replied, standing up. "I should probably get to bed. This has been a long day."

Amanda rose quickly. "Oh, sure. I'm sorry. I should have shown you to your room. Thanks for staying. I feel much safer with you here."

Jim walked closer to her and looking into her eyes, he said, "I'm glad to be here."

Amanda felt her body go limp, as if she were going to fall right into his arms. She didn't need to though, because he reached out and embraced her. It was the most passionate hug she'd ever felt, and she felt tears forming in her eyes. Jim slowly released her, and they looked at each other lovingly.

"After my life goes back to normal," he said, "I hope we can spend quality time getting to know each other."

"That would be nice," Amanda said, almost automatically.

He picked up his suitcase, and she led him to his room, wishing she could join him, too. "Good-night. Let me know if you need anything," she said, turning to leave.

Jim yawned. "Will do."

After letting out the dog and resetting the alarm system, Amanda went to bed as well. She suddenly realized how tired she was, and just as her head hit the pillow, she fell asleep.

They woke up at various times the next morning. Amanda was first. It was Tuesday, and she was still in the habit of getting up early as if she were going into an office. She showered and got dressed quickly, hoping Jim and Karen didn't get up until she'd had a cup of coffee alone with quiet thoughts. As good luck would have it, she got her wish. She was able to drink an entire cup before Karen came into the kitchen still wearing her robe. Amanda motioned for her to come sit at the table.

"Good morning," Karen said, yawning. "Jim got to the shower before I did, so I thought I'd come in to talk to you."

"How'd you sleep?"

"Not bad, but I did have a nightmare about a man chasing me through the woods. It was probably because I was scared after the break-in and Hank's beating."

"It probably was. This entire situation makes no sense. I still can't figure out why anyone would terrorize people over genealogy research."

"I know. It's very disturbing, but I think your idea about hiring a PI is a good one."

"It seems to be the best option at this point if you want to get to the bottom of this. Would you like some coffee?"

"I'd love some."

Amanda pulled a large brown mug from the cabinet and filled it to the brim with coffee. Handing it to Karen, she asked, "Would you like milk and sugar in it?"

"Oh, no. I never put anything in my coffee."

Amanda smiled, remembering how her grandpa taught her to drink it. His words reverberated in her mind—*You have to drink it black with me, kid. No cream or sugar allowed.*

Karen smiled and blew into her mug, and then took a sip. "Perfect cup."

"Thanks. I've had a lot of experience. Would you like some cereal?"

"If it's no bother—I certainly would."

"No problem at all," Amanda said, handing her a box of granola. "I'll set out everything, so Jim can have some, too." She then set the table with bowls and spoons and placed a carton of milk in the middle.

Amanda poured herself another cup of coffee and sat down next to Karen. "Anyway, as we were discussing—I think a private investigator is the way to go, and I know one who seems to be trustworthy."

"Who is it?"

"His name is Mike Kennedy. He sometimes came into the clinic to ask questions. Even though we never gave him any information, he was always polite and understanding."

"Should we contact him today?"

"Let's ask Jim when he gets out of the shower."

"Ask me what?"

They turned to see Jim standing in the kitchen.

"We're thinking of calling a PI today, if it's okay with you," Karen responded.

"Sure. I know I wasn't enthused about that, but we might as well try it. We don't have any other ideas, unless we snoop around ourselves, and something tells me that wouldn't be a good idea."

"I agree," Amanda said. "Snooping around ourselves has proven to be dangerous up to this point. I know a guy we can call today."

"Let's do it this morning," Jim said. "I plan to go home this afternoon to check on the house."

"I'll go with you," Karen offered.

"Are you sure?"

"Positive."

"Good, but let's eat first," Amanda said, taking a bite of cereal.

"Sounds like a good idea to me," Jim said, as he sat down in the chair next to her.

They talked, ate, and drank coffee for over an hour until Karen announced she was going to take a shower. "I'll be back soon, so we can call the PI," she said, picking up her plate to put it in the dishwasher.

"Oh, don't bother with that. I'll get it," Amanda said.

Karen was hesitant. "Are you sure?"

"Absolutely."

After she departed and Jim finished his coffee, Amanda began clearing away the dishes. Jim tried to help, but she insisted it was faster if he didn't. He then said he could at least take Bandy outside, and she agreed to that. She used the time to thoroughly wipe down the table and counters, until they returned about twenty minutes later.

"Wow. It's cold out there," Jim announced, shutting the door quickly. Amanda noticed his cheeks were flushed. Bandy, on the other hand, held her tail high and appeared to be quite exhilarated.

"I noticed you didn't wear a coat, so I'm sure it wasn't very comfortable."

"Did I tell you I hate winter?"

"No, but I'm in complete agreement with you on that."

Jim nodded and changed the subject. "We need to get our Thanksgiving plans in order."

"Would you like to have it here instead of your house now that you've had a break-in?" Amanda asked.

"I'll consider that. I'm dreading going back there today to clean up the mess."

"Let's have it at my house. I insist. It will do you good to stay away from there as much as possible."

Jim smiled. "Thanks. I'll take you up on that, and I don't believe Karen will mind."

"It will be casual. No stress. I promise."

Chapter 11

They walked into the office to wait for Karen, and Amanda pulled Mike Kennedy's business card from her desk drawer. "Glad I saved this," she said, waving the card at Jim.

"I hope he can help."

"If he can't, then we'll keep searching, but we'll be more discreet about it than we have been."

"And that's one of the things I like about you, Amanda. You always have an idea or a solution in case something doesn't work."

She smiled sheepishly. "Thanks. I try." A silence fell between them until Karen walked into the room.

"That feels better," she said. "A hot shower always wakes me up."

Amanda nodded. "Are you ready to call the PI?"

"Certainly," Karen replied.

Amanda punched the number into her mobile phone and waited for it to connect. She didn't know if Mike would answer, so she was prepared to leave a message. As luck would have it, he picked up his phone.

"Hi, Mike. It's Amanda Latham. I was a social worker at a clinic in Kansas City, and we spoke on several occasions."

"Ah, yes, Amanda. I remember you well. You were always polite to me—unlike some of the others at that clinic who shunned me."

"I thought you were professional and trying to do your job, which I can only imagine, was difficult in some cases."

"Boy, was it ever. But you didn't call me to reminisce now, did you?"

"You're right. Good deduction, and that's why you're a PI and I'm not," Amanda joked. "I've been involved with a troubling case, and I hope you can be of service."

"Anything for you. What is it?"

"I'm going to put you on speaker, if that's okay, because there are a couple of other people here who need to tell you about it."

"That's fine. With whom will I be speaking?"

She put the phone on speaker, and then responded, "Jim Dorion and his sister, Karen."

"Pleased to meet you," Mike said.

"Likewise," Jim responded.

"Me, too," Karen added.

"What can I do for you?" Mike asked.

"We need to find out who threatened us and broke into our home," Jim answered. "But first, let me provide you with the background information."

"That would be great."

Jim gave him a brief account of the details—the near-murder of Margarethe, the letter from Hans that Phillip mentioned, and the threats made to the family in the past. He then described the phone call he received, as well as the break-in, the stolen genealogy folder, and Hank's beating.

"This is quite interesting, indeed," Mike responded. "Hold on a minute while I finish typing this into my file."

They all remained quiet, and several minutes passed before Mike asked a question that Jim and Karen probably didn't want to answer. "Where does Amanda fit into all of this? I mean, how did she become involved since she's not a family member?"

Karen nodded at Jim. "Are you sure?" he whispered.

Karen then spoke loudly toward the phone. "I'll answer that one for you, Mike," she said. "We came to see Amanda for a counseling session because I was having nightmares that were interfering with my daily life. It was getting to the point where I could barely function because I was always anxious. Amanda suggested we research our family's history. She wondered if I was experiencing ancestral trauma. As Jim just mentioned, we found out that our great-great-grandmother, Margarethe, had been beaten nearly to death by her husband. As if this wasn't disturbing enough, we found out that the man was released from prison early. Margarethe had married our great-great-grandfather, Hans Mueller, by that point. She had several children with him, but she later disappeared. As Jim said, we began to research further and found a distant relative named Phillip Mueller, who has enlightened us on some of the history and the threats made to the family in the past. And, as Jim also mentioned, Phillip shared a letter with us which states that it was suspected that Margarethe was pushed over a cliff into a river."

Mike interrupted. "Do you have a copy of the letter?"

"We'll have one soon. It's been mailed by Phillip, but I haven't picked up our mail," Jim responded.

"Do you think the person or persons who broke into your house were searching for a document like that?"

"I'm going to take a guess that there were a couple of people involved, and I don't know if they were searching for anything. I assumed they were merely trying to scare us."

"But you said that they stole a genealogy folder."

"Good point. Now, I'm wondering if they *were* looking for a document of some kind."

"Is your mailbox the type that locks?" Mike asked.

"Yes, it is, and I don't think it's been disturbed. It's located up the block, along with everyone else's on our street. Our address isn't on the outside of the box, so I doubt anyone could have figured out which one to break into."

"That's good," Mike said. "Have you cleaned your house since the break-in?"

"No, we haven't," Jim responded.

"Would you mind if I met you there, so I can see everything before you clean it up?"

"No problem."

"Okay. I'll see you there. What's your address?"

Jim provided the information.

"I assume you're taking the case, Mike?" Amanda questioned.

"I am, indeed."

"Okay, we'll meet you at my house," Jim confirmed. "Please give us at least forty-five minutes to get there."

"It doesn't matter if it takes you longer. I want to arrive early, so I can observe your street."

"Understood."

"All right, then. Thanks, Mike," Amanda said.

"Yes, thank you," Karen added.

Amanda cut the connection. "I guess you'd better get going. I have a feeling he'll be there in a matter of five minutes."

"You should come with us," Karen suggested.

Jim nodded. "Yes, why don't you?"

"Sure. I'll follow you there, so you don't need to drive me home."

Jim shook his head. "Just ride with us. I'd rather you not come home alone—just in case."

"Okay. Go ahead and pack up while I take out the dog."

The Dorions packed their suitcases, and Karen again insisted that Amanda ride in the front seat of the car. They pulled out of the driveway several minutes later and traveled north for thirty minutes before heading east. Unfortunately, they had to stop at a railroad crossing because a slow-moving train was creeping along the tracks. Jim joked that it would be their luck that it would stop in front of them. Finally, the caboose rumbled past, and the crossing arms lifted.

"And that's why I told Mike it would take forty-five minutes to get there," Jim said, as they slowly crossed the bumpy tracks.

Amanda snickered. "I think Mike wanted us to be late, so he could nose around. It probably makes him feel like more of a sleuth."

"I got that impression, too," Karen agreed, smiling.

They continued traveling east for another ten minutes, and then Jim announced they were almost there. He turned south into a neighborhood with beautiful houses and large yards.

"Nice neighborhood," Amanda commented.

"Thanks," Jim said. He slowed down as he approached a stone and brick French country style home, and then turned into the driveway. There was a tall blue spruce anchoring one side of the façade and a maple tree on the other. The brick porch was surrounded by holly bushes.

"Wow!" Amanda said. "Your house is gorgeous."

"It belonged to our parents, and we decided not to sell it after they died. The amount of inheritance they left allowed us to keep it. Karen lived here alone for a long time after our parents died, and I lived in a condo in Kansas City. I decided to sell my place and move in after she became more anxious."

"I'm sorry you had to sell your condo," Karen said quietly. "I know I've been a burden."

"Don't say that," Jim said. "You have never been a burden. We're family. I'd do anything for you, and I'm glad to be here."

"Thanks. I'm glad, too."

"Well, the house is absolutely lovely," Amanda said.

"Thank you," Karen said, turning to look out the back window. "Do you see Mike anywhere?"

Jim stopped the car in the driveway, so they could see if he was nearby.

"There he is," Amanda said, pointing up the road to a man walking near the post that housed the community mailboxes. Mike was not threatening in appearance—small in stature with medium brown hair and a large mustache. Amanda smiled to herself, remembering how it curled into a scroll-like shape on each side of his face. She wondered if the mustache had ever attracted attention when he was out sleuthing around. That was something no PI would want if they were trying to be sneaky. However, as she watched Mike walking up the road, she realized that she probably wouldn't have suspected him of doing anything of a covert nature. He appeared to be on a leisurely walk like a regular guy in the neighborhood.

Mike waved as he walked toward them, and then promptly tripped and fell to his knees. He rose quickly and brushed off his khaki trousers, but he didn't seem embarrassed at all. In fact, he was smiling. Amanda remembered that he sometimes bumped into things and tripped over his own feet whenever he came into the clinic, which was part of the reason why she liked him. He always seemed so humble. While others might have taken him for a bumbling fool after witnessing his mannerisms, she knew he was a man who was always deep in thought—the type of person who would solve a case. Jim glanced at her and shook his head. "Don't worry," she said. "He's good."

"Okay," he said hesitantly. He then clicked the garage door opener and parked the car inside. Amanda and Karen climbed out of the car and stretched, and Jim pulled the suitcases from the trunk. He set them aside, and they stood in the driveway and waited for Mike.

"Hello, there!" Amanda said as he approached. "It's nice to see you, and I'm so glad you took the case." She noticed that his mustache now had a few streaks of gray running through it.

"Great to see you, too," Mike said. "This is indeed an interesting one." He extended his hand to Jim and then to Karen. "It's a pleasure to meet both of you."

"We're glad you're here," Karen said, smiling. "Where did you park?"

"My car is parked up the road. I thought it would be better that way in case someone is watching your house."

Jim didn't overtly express his approval of Mike's presence, but he said, "I hope you can help us."

"I do, too. I've looked at the mailboxes on your street, and none of them appear to have been tampered with, so hopefully that letter is in there."

"I'll check on it," Jim said. "Did you see how they broke into the house?"

"I have not. I wanted to walk around to check out the neighborhood and the mailboxes first."

They went inside through the garage entrance, which was a small hallway that led to the kitchen. It was a bright and cheery room with yellow painted walls. The cabinets were painted white and the counters were made of black granite. Large windows lined the back of the house, which backed to the east. This provided a nice view of the backyard, which had a creek running through it and a lot of trees. There was also a nice outdoor building, which Amanda knew probably held lawncare equipment and tools.

"I love your kitchen and backyard," she said. "How many acres do you have here?"

"Thanks," Jim said. "It's just one acre, but it's very private. The nearest house is far across the creek. That's probably why someone was able to break in here without being noticed." He pointed to the back door, which had a board covering where the glass would have been. "I put up the board when I left here yesterday."

Mike went to the door and carefully inspected it. "An all-glass door is an easy target, but it makes a lot of noise when someone breaks one. The person who did this either knew you weren't home, or they didn't care."

"Glad we *weren't* here," Karen said.

Jim led them to the office, which was near the front door. They waded through papers scattered across the floor—thanks to the drawers being yanked from the desk. However, Mike was most interested in the smashed computer. He stood looking down at it, twirling the right side of his mustache with his fingers. "Did you have anything on there that someone might have wanted?" he asked.

"Just my work stuff—boring emails about information technology consulting projects."

"We had our genealogy information on there, too," Karen added.

"Is there a password on the computer?"

"Yes. We each have our own," Jim replied.

Mike nodded as he pulled a small notepad and pen from his jacket pocket. "You said that a genealogy folder is missing. Where was it located?"

"It was a red folder, and it was on top of the desk on the right side. I don't know why the intruders felt the need to yank out the drawers and smash the computer."

Mike scribbled on his notepad. "I'd say that was for a dramatic effect, and perhaps they were looking for more things. Show me the other rooms that were vandalized, and then we'll talk about what was inside the genealogy folder."

"Sure," Karen said. "I'll lead you to my room, so you can see what was done to my bed."

Mike followed her down the hall with Amanda and Jim trailing close behind. Karen paused for a bit before entering her room, as if she had to get her courage up before seeing it again. Mike quickly marched inside and stood by the bed. He began to twirl his mustache again as he pointed to the slashed bedding. "It looks like someone was trying to send a message of fear here." He motioned toward the drawers that were pulled out. "I'm assuming the intruders did that and you aren't a slovenly sloth."

Karen smiled. "Of course, they did that. Goodness. I don't know what they could have been searching for in here."

"It's always difficult to guess," Mike said.

"I'll show you my room," Jim said, motioning for everyone to follow. "They slashed my bedding, too."

Mike's right shoulder bumped against the doorway when he entered the room, but he ignored it and surveyed the area. "They were definitely sending a warning," he said, scribbling on his notepad.

Jim's eyes narrowed as he spoke. "Well, it's certainly a sick sort of warning, but I'm not stopping our family research. No one is going to intimidate me.

If anything, they've just made me want to search our history even more. There must be something in our past they want to be kept a secret. Not happening. I don't care what it takes to discover the truth—I want to know." Jim then turned and walked back toward the office. Everyone followed without speaking.

It was the first time Amanda had ever seen such fire in his eyes. She didn't blame him, but she was worried about Karen. Jim must have been, too, because he turned to her and said, "Karen, I hope you're with me on this."

"I am, but I'm afraid we're in danger."

Amanda said, "Both of you are welcome to stay with me until this is sorted out."

"I appreciate that," Karen responded. "I was thinking of being at home tonight, but after coming here today, I'm going to take you up on the offer."

"I'll drive you back to Amanda's, and then I'm returning here to clean up the house after Mike has a chance to go through it," Jim said.

"That reminds me. Will you go get your mail, so I can see the letter you mentioned?" Mike asked.

"Absolutely. I nearly forgot about that," Jim replied. He went to the entryway table and pulled a key out of a drawer. "I'll be back in a minute," he called, walking out the door.

Amanda and Karen stood in the entryway near the office, while Mike inspected what was left of the computer.

"I need to know what was in that genealogy folder," he said, looking at Karen.

"There wasn't much in it, really. Just names— beginning with our great-great-grandparents, Hans and Margarethe Mueller. I added a notation next to Margarethe indicating that she was probably pushed into a river by Albert Kleiner. Below Hans and

Margarethe, we listed their children—one of whom was our great-grandfather Johann Mueller. They had a daughter named Sophia. Phillip told us he has family records that indicate she was killed by her husband. I made a notation of this in the folder. Johann was the father of our maternal grandmother, Anna, who married Friedrich Rohr. They were the parents of our mother, Katerina, who married Henry Dorion."

Mike appeared to be deep in thought as he stood behind the desk and twirled the right side of his mustache. "You only had your mother's side of the family listed in the folder. Is that correct?"

"Yes. We listed our father as Henry Dorion, but we hadn't written anything about his side of the family yet."

"It does appear that all of this is linked to your research into the Mueller family history. Now, we need to find out why. That will be my job, and I'm going to make it my mission. This is one of the most interesting cases I've seen for quite some time."

Chapter 12

At that moment, Jim opened the front door with an envelope in his hand. "Here's the letter! I guess we should open it now." He reached into his front pocket and pulled out a small folding knife, then carefully cut a slit on the top of the envelope. As he pulled out the letter, everyone gathered around him. The cursive script displayed beautiful penmanship from an era when people took pride in their handwriting.

"I'll read it out loud," Jim announced. He cleared his throat and began to read.

Dear Reverend Kaefer:

I trust that everything is going as it should be there, and I pray the children are all okay. Thank you for taking care of them and for keeping them out of harm's way. There is not a day that goes by that I don't think of each of them with an aching heart. Now, I must inform you of some tragic news. Margarethe is missing, and I presume she was killed. I am certain she was pushed off a bluff into the Mississippi River by a man named Albert Kleiner. I've heard this from someone in town, who says he saw it happen. Albert is the one who began a letter-writing campaign to get the governor to release her former husband from prison. The Kleiner family has had a vendetta against my wife's family since they lived in Germany. There was a battle over land ownership, and then Albert Kleiner made advances toward Margarethe. She pushed him away, and now I fear, he has pushed her into the river. I've reported her disappearance to the local police, and they've questioned Albert, but they let him go. There is no evidence because Margarethe's body has not been found. The witness who saw her being pushed is a known drinker in town. The police don't believe him because of his nearly constant state of drunkenness, and they also don't believe Albert would commit a crime such as this. I've confronted Albert, and he laughed and said Margarethe had it coming to her. We got into a fight, but some of his friends broke it up. They also threatened that they would kill my children if they ever found them. I believe you can see why it would be best if they remained with you. I am forever in your debt.

    Hans Mueller

Everyone was quiet for a moment, taking in what they'd just heard, until Mike cleared his throat to speak. "Just to be clear, this letter has been in the possession of a distant relative named Phillip Mueller. Is that correct?"

"Yes," Jim answered. "Phillip's grandfather, Ernst, was the brother of our great-grandfather Johann. They were the sons of Hans and Margarethe. Reverend Kaefer raised the kids, due to the threats made toward the family, and Ernst found the letter inside of a drawer in the preacher's bedroom."

"When you were getting the mail, Karen also mentioned that there was a girl named Sophia. Did Hans and Margarethe have any other children besides Ernst, Johann, and Sophia?" Mike asked.

"Yes. They had another son named Albrecht, who was killed during World War I."

Mike scratched his head, and then said, "Karen mentioned that Sophia might have been murdered. Tell me more about what you've heard about that."

Jim nodded. "We only know what Phillip told us. He said that his grandpa Ernst documented that Sophia was killed by her husband—that he forced her to drink poison. At Sophia's funeral, her husband confessed to Ernst that he had done it. However, no one would believe it, because he came from a well-to-do family."

"I see," Mike said. "What was the name of Sophia's husband?"

"Thomas Johnson," Karen announced.

"And you said that you made a notation of the suspected murder in the genealogy folder that was stolen, right?"

"Yes," Karen replied.

"Hmm. Sorry. I just needed to hear that again to make sure I have this down correctly," Mike said, writing furiously.

"What are you thinking?" Jim asked.

"I'm not sure what to think yet, but perhaps the circumstances surrounding Sophia's death might be something to look into further. I'd also like to know more about Hank. You mentioned on the phone that he was badly beaten. I also saw that story on the news. What were the circumstances leading up to it?"

Jim provided the details about how the database had instructions—that a phone number was to be called and a code entered if anyone asked questions about Sophia, and that after calling, Hank was instructed to never tell anyone about it.

"And I believe he was attacked because he told us about it when we returned," Jim added.

"Was he beaten up the same day after you left?"

"Unfortunately, yes. Amanda saw it on the news that evening. Karen and I came home to the aftermath of the break-in on that evening as well."

"Did you see anything suspicious when you left the cemetery?"

Amanda nodded, and then said, "We saw a nice dark-blue sedan with tinted windows—probably a Lincoln or Cadillac—parked on the street. We couldn't see if anyone was inside though, and we didn't get the tag number."

"I doubt it's uncommon for a dark-colored sedan to be parked near a cemetery. However, given what happened to Hank at around the same time, there might be a connection," Mike explained.

"There's something else," Karen said. "We also found that the database in the cemetery had a code listed next to each Mueller name—not just Sophia's. The code number was the year they were born. For instance, Sophia's code number was 1882, which was her date of birth. Hank did a preliminary search on some other surnames, but there were no codes listed for anyone outside of the Mueller family."

"That is very odd. Are there any leads in Hank's case?"

"Not that we know of yet," Amanda answered. "Hank wasn't able to talk very long, due to his injuries. He said that two large bald guys came into the office. They told him they were going to teach him a lesson so he'd keep his mouth shut, and then they started beating him. He pretended to be knocked out, and they stopped. That was when he heard one of the men say that Simon would be pleased."

Mike's eyes lit up. "So, they showed their faces and they mentioned a name? Either they are the dumbest criminals ever or they're sure nothing will happen to them if they get caught. Hold on just a second while I write this down."

Amanda, Karen, and Jim exchanged glances while Mike wrote down the information. It was then that Amanda had her first twinge of feeling exhausted, and she yawned out loud. "Sorry," she whispered.

Mike put his notepad and pen back inside his pocket. "I'm sure you're all probably tired, so I'll get out of here. Let me know if you think of anything else that might help—otherwise, I'll get back to you when I sort out some things."

Jim extended his hand. "Thanks, and we look forward to hearing from you. Is it okay to clean up the mess now, or do you think you'll need to go through it again?"

"You can clean up. Also, please call me if you find anything else missing."

"Will do."

Amanda held up her forefinger and said, "One more thing. I did some research on Albert Kleiner, and it appears he was an ancestor of Senator Bart Kleiner."

Mike arched his eyebrows. "That is interesting. I'll check that out."

"I hope you can find answers for us," Karen said.

"Oh, I will find at least some of the answers," Mike said confidently, now twirling the left side of his mustache. "You folks get some rest, and I'll do the detective work."

Jim looked as if he'd just remembered something important. "I didn't ask. What's your fee for something like this?"

"That's funny. I forgot about that. I'd like a retainer of $100.00, which will be applied toward my $40.00 hourly rate."

"No problem. Do you take a debit card? I rarely use checks anymore."

"I sure do. Hold on a minute while I get the card reader out of my car," Mike said, walking toward the door. He returned shortly and completed the transaction.

As soon as Mike left, Jim said, "I must admit that I had my doubts about him when I saw him stumbling up the road, but he's very sharp."

"I like him," Karen announced. "He seems sincere."

"I've always thought that, too," Amanda agreed. "He's also extremely focused on getting the facts straight, and I know he'll give your case all of his attention."

Jim nodded. "That's just what we need."

"I'm so tired," Karen said. "We should head back to Amanda's now."

"I agree. Let's get going," Jim said.

Amanda looked at Jim. "Are you still spending the night here after you drop us off?"

"Yes, I think it's best. I doubt I'll sleep, so I'll work all night to clean up the mess."

"I don't want you to do it alone," Karen said, looking around the room. "Maybe I should stay home tonight instead of going to Amanda's."

"I can do it. I'd rather you get some rest."

Karen didn't argue about it. "Okay," she said, walking toward her bedroom. "I'm going to leave my suitcase here and pack a smaller bag to take with me for the night."

They arrived at Amanda's home at around half past four in the afternoon. Everything looked secure, and Bandy barked loudly as soon as they walked inside. Amanda quickly keyed in the code for the alarm system, and Jim announced he was going to check out each room to make sure no one was hiding under a bed or in a closet. He wasn't armed though, so Amanda wondered what he'd do if he came upon an intruder. As soon as Jim announced that all was clear, he took Bandy outside with him to check out the perimeter of the house. There was no sign that anyone had tampered with anything, so he came back inside.

"Everything looks fine," he said, patting Bandy's head.

"I'm glad," Amanda said. "Would you like to eat before you leave?"

"I'm not that hungry, so I'll just grab a quick bite later."

"I know what you mean. I'm not hungry either."

"Ditto that," Karen added.

"Okay, then. I'll text or call you in the morning," Jim announced, walking toward the front door.

Amanda thought he looked a bit worried, but she didn't blame him. "Talk to you later," she said.

Karen patted him on the arm. "Please try to sleep."

"I will," he assured.

Amanda set the alarm system after Jim was gone. Even though she knew Karen wasn't hungry, she thought she should still offer her something to eat. "I know it's early, but I can make a snack if you'd like."

Karen hesitated a bit, and then nodded. "I think a bowl of cereal would coat my stomach for the night."

"Are you sure? You had cereal for breakfast today."

"Honestly, that's all I want."

"Okay, then I'll have some, too."

Amanda fed Bandy first, and then prepared the bowls of cereal. Karen poured a couple of glasses of water, and they sat at the table to eat.

"This hits the spot," Karen said.

"Same," Amanda agreed. "I'm going to watch TV, and then go to bed early. Is there anything you like to see on Tuesday nights?"

"Not really. I usually play around on my tablet while Jim watches news channels."

"Did you bring your tablet?"

"Yes, it's in my bag."

"I'm glad the intruder didn't steal or smash it."

"Me, too. I was surprised about that. I have some genealogy information on it that I've emailed to myself as I've done searches."

"Well, you're welcome to bring it to the great room while I watch TV. I want you to feel at home."

"Thanks. I appreciate that."

Amanda turned on the television while she retrieved her tablet. She was glad Karen was staying, because she didn't want to be alone—not that she was afraid. The house felt active again, and for that reason, she felt a twinge of contentment. At 8:45, Karen announced she was going to bed, and Amanda decided to do the same. She let Bandy out one last time for the day, and then went to her room with the hound following close behind.

Amanda awoke at around eight o'clock on Wednesday morning, which made her feel a bit disoriented. She was accustomed to getting up a couple of hours earlier, but she knew she must have needed the extra sleep. After feeding the dog, she started the coffee pot before taking a shower. She returned to the kitchen dressed and ready for the day, and Karen shuffled in a few minutes later, looking quite rested.

"You look like you slept well," Amanda observed.

Karen smiled. "I feel much better."

"No nightmares?"

"Not a one. In fact, I didn't even dream at all. I feel at peace in this house."

"I do, too, which is why I decided to move back here as soon as it went on the market."

"Do you miss them?"

Amanda knew what Karen meant, but she didn't respond as such. "Them?"

"Your grandparents. Do you miss them?"

"Every day. I must admit, if I could go back in time to spend just one day of my life as I see fit, I'd spend it here with them. I'd drink coffee with my grandfather, and I'd follow my grandmother around the farm to feed the chickens and care for the horses."

"You don't have any other pets here except your dog. Have you thought about getting other animals?"

"Not at this point. It's a lot to take care of when you're alone. It's hard enough for me to keep the pasture mowed, and sometimes the tractor breaks down."

"I can't imagine you on a tractor."

"It was the first four-wheel vehicle I ever drove. My grandfather let me drive his when I was in elementary school."

"Wow. I'll bet that was fun."

Amanda snickered. "It was, until I decided to wave at some boys and hit a fence. Grandpa was not happy at all. It only scratched the tractor a little bit, but I was more careful after that."

"Do you still have it?"

"No. My grandfather sold it a long time ago. Unfortunately, the tractor I use now isn't as good as the old one."

"That's too bad."

"Would you like something to eat? I can make some toast and eggs if you're tired of cereal."

"That sounds great. I can make it though."

"Go for it," Amanda said, pointing to the bread on the counter.

"Thanks."

Amanda was happy Karen seemed to be so comfortable but still worried that she might be attempting to hide an internal struggle due to the recent events. "So, how are you doing these days with everything that's been going on?" she asked, taking a seat at the table.

Karen walked to the counter and took the twist tie off the loaf of bread. "I'm not happy about the threatening phone call and the break-in, but I'm feeling better. And even though life has taken a weird turn, I still feel less fear than before. I believe that part of feeling more at peace is due to the search for Margarethe because I've felt involved in solving the mystery."

"Well, I'm very glad you're feeling more at peace."

"I also think you've helped a lot, because you've taken me seriously. I went to a lot of therapists before coming to see you, and I felt like they were patronizing me."

"I didn't do much. You're stronger than you think, Karen. A therapist that's right for one person, might not be a good fit for another. Just promise me you'll find one you like if you start feeling badly again. I'm here if you need someone to talk to as a friend—but remember, I'm out of the picture if you need a therapist."

"I understand. I'd rather be your friend than your client anyway," Karen said, smiling.

"I like that better, too."

Karen finished making her breakfast before joining Amanda at the table. They drank coffee and talked until their phones vibrated with a group text from Jim. He said he'd finished cleaning and was waiting for the glass company to arrive to install a new panel on the back door. He said he'd drive to Amanda's after the installer left, and he wanted to know if everything was okay. They responded with a "thumbs up" emoji and let him know they were fine. Karen cleared away her breakfast dishes and announced she was going to take a shower.

Chapter 13

Amanda went outside on the deck with Bandy to get some fresh air. As she exhaled, a misty cloud appeared, serving as visible proof that the temperature was indeed low. However, the sun was shining, which always brightened her mood. She knew the upcoming winter months would be long in Kansas and felt as if she were perpetually waiting for spring—even during the summer months. Spring represented promise and hope, and it was the sense of renewal she craved. Her thoughts turned to Thanksgiving, and for the first time in years, she felt excited about the holiday.

She realized she was shivering and whistled for Bandy to come back inside with her. She also thought it would be a good time to call the hospital to check on Hank. The front desk quickly connected her to his room, and she was relieved that he answered cheerfully.

"Hello, Hank! It's Amanda. I hope you're doing better. We've all been worried about you."

"I'm doing fine. My friend, Debbie Blake, will take me home today as soon as the doctors say it's okay. Well…actually…not home. She's taking me to her house to stay for a few days. I still have headaches, and they've been monitoring my heart. Strange thing. It might be a mixed blessing that I had to come to the hospital, because the doctors found out I had a clogged artery to my heart. I was on the verge of an attack. They put in a stent and fixed me, so I'm almost as good as new."

"That's such a relief. I'm glad they caught it."

"Yeah, and my son flew here from Minnesota to see me in the hospital. He doesn't get too much time off work, so it was nice to see him."

"You can't beat that. Oops, I'm sorry. I shouldn't have worded it like that," Amanda said.

"That's okay. I didn't think anything of it."

"Do you think you're going to go back to work at the cemetery?"

"Not right away, and my son doesn't think I should go back there at all."

"I wouldn't blame you."

"I might come volunteer here at the hospital instead."

"That sounds like a good idea. I'll bet they'd be thrilled to have you there."

"I hope so."

"Is there anything we can do for you? Jim and Karen and I feel bad about what happened."

"I don't need anything. It's not your fault, so don't beat yourself up over it," Hank said, snickering.

"Well, I'm glad you have your sense of humor. I don't know that I would."

"When you get to be my age, you'll find that humor helps in many situations."

"I believe that."

"By the way, did your friends ever find the information they needed on their family?"

"They're still searching, and they've now hired a private investigator. Someone broke into their house and ransacked it on the same day as you were beaten up. We told Officer Crenshaw all about it when we came to see you in the hospital. I doubt you'd remember that though."

"I vaguely remember you being here, but things are a bit fuzzy."

"Understandable. Anyway, that's what's going on."

"I hope the private investigator can sort things out. I still have Jim's business card, so I'll let you know if I find out anything."

"You should probably lie low on this. I don't want you to get hurt again. However, would you be willing to talk to the PI if he wants to ask you a few questions?"

"I would do that. I'll give you my mobile number, as well as Debbie's address in case you need to reach me."

"That would be great. Thank you so much," Amanda said. She reached into her utility drawer and pulled out a pen and small piece of paper. She wrote quickly as Hank provided the information.

"I hope to see you again," Hank said.

"I do, too. Good-bye for now," Amanda said.

Karen entered the room as she clicked off the phone. "Anything new?"

"I decided to call and check on Hank," Amanda said as she put his information into the drawer.

"Is he okay?"

"Better than ever. The doctors found a clogged artery to his heart and put in a stent. He probably would have had a heart attack if he hadn't gone to the hospital when he did."

"Wow. That's unreal. In a weird way, it's good he had to be admitted."

"He said the same thing. I hope we don't need to contact him again, but I'm afraid Mike will want to ask him some questions."

"He probably will," Karen sighed. "I don't want to put Hank in further jeopardy, but if talking to Mike helps find out who did this, then it must be done."

Amanda nodded, and then changed the subject. "We should take a walk outside before Jim gets here. It's cold, but the fresh air will do us good."

"That sounds wonderful. I'll go get my coat."

"I'd better get mine, too."

Amanda retrieved her jacket from the hall closet and waited for Karen to return with hers. They exited through the back door, but she didn't lock it since they'd be close enough to see if anyone approached. Although Bandy stayed nearby, she explored several areas with her nose as they walked. Amanda showed Karen the barn, which once held several horses, and then they walked on into the pasture. She talked about gathering pecans in November, and how she'd sit with her grandmother to crack them in preparation for pecan pies on Thanksgiving. There was an abundance of the nuts scattered on the ground.

"Don't you pick them up anymore?" Karen asked.

Amanda was slightly embarrassed. She'd forgotten to come out to gather them. "You know—I should do that. Do you want to go to the shed with me to get the wheelbarrow?"

"I'd love to."

"I'll get the key first. It's in the laundry room hanging on a hook," Amanda said as they walked back toward the house.

After retrieving the key, she led Karen to the shed near an abandoned chicken coop. Pointing to it, she said, "That's where we kept the chickens. Grandma and I would get up early in the morning, so we could gather eggs."

"That would be fun," Karen said.

"It was—sometimes—unless there was a big black snake in there. They liked to eat the eggs, and Grandma and I usually ran from the coop when we saw one. They won't hurt you though. It's the copperheads you need to watch out for when you're walking. They are poisonous, but they're usually not out this time of the year."

Karen looked down at her feet as if she were afraid she'd step on one. "I'm familiar with copperheads. We've seen one near our house, and I'm not a fan of snakes of any kind."

Amanda unlocked the shed, opened the door, and pulled out the wheelbarrow. "I haven't used this for a while. This will be fun."

"I think we should use some of the pecans for a pie this Thanksgiving," Karen said.

Amanda felt her eyes sting as tears began to form. "I'd like that," she said, blocking her emotions from surfacing. She'd always been rather stoic, especially around others. But the anticipation of gathering pecans for the holiday reminded her of how much she missed her grandparents. They took turns pushing the wheelbarrow through the pasture until they reached the patch of scattered nuts. The bright sun took some of the chill out of the autumn air, which made for a pleasant day to be outside. Soon the wheelbarrow was filled with pecans, and they pushed it back toward the house.

"That was fun," Karen said. "Do you have any other chores we could do?"

Amanda smiled. She was glad to be with someone who was excited about doing things outside. "Not right now, but I'm sure I'll think of something later."

As they approached the house, Amanda noticed Jim's Subaru in the driveway. He quickly climbed out when he saw them. "There you are! I was worried when no one answered the door, and Bandy didn't bark either."

"We decided to go pick up pecans, and the dog went with us," Karen announced.

"I wonder where she went," Amanda said, looking around. "We were having so much fun that I didn't even notice she'd disappeared." She whistled, and Bandy came running toward them.

"Well-trained dog," Jim said.

Amanda snickered. "She just thinks she's getting a treat."

Jim bent down and patted Bandy on the head. "That's okay, girl. I'll give you something." He then winked at Amanda, and she smiled and shook her head.

They went inside the house, and it didn't escape Jim's notice that the back door hadn't been locked. "You really should keep things locked up. You don't want to come inside to an intruder."

Amanda rolled her eyes. "I know. I know. We weren't that far away, and I thought it would be okay. Besides, the front door is locked. We came out through the back door, and I didn't think anyone would attempt to come in that way."

"I'm going to check around just in case."

"If you feel it's necessary."

"I do."

Amanda and Karen waited just inside the back door while Jim checked each room of the house. He returned with a good report. Nothing had been disturbed, and no one was hiding under any of the beds or lurking in a closet. Amanda felt rather foolish for leaving the door unlocked, but she wasn't accustomed to living in fear.

Karen changed the subject as they walked into the kitchen. "Amanda called and checked on Hank this morning. He's doing much better."

"That's good news. I'm so glad," Jim said, and then added, "I promised the dog a treat, so I'd better do that."

Amanda reached into a cabinet and pulled out the jar of dog biscuits. She handed one to Jim, but he made Bandy lift her paw and shake his hand before he gave it to her. She then trotted off with her tail held high.

"Did you get the glass replaced on your door?" Amanda asked, putting the jar back into the cabinet.

"Yes. It didn't take long at all, and I cleaned the entire house, too."

"That's good, but I'm sure that wasn't much fun."

Karen said, "Thanks for doing that. I'll come back home tonight."

"You don't have to if you don't want to," Jim responded.

"I think it's important that I do. That way, if anyone is watching, they'll know they didn't scare us enough to flee the house."

Jim looked at Amanda and said, "I really don't want to leave you here alone."

"Honestly, I'm fine. I have an alarm system and a dog, and I live in a rural area. Plus, I'm not part of the family, so I doubt I'm at risk. I think you should invest in an alarm system for your house though. I can't believe you don't have one."

"It's on my list of things to do, but I got too busy today. In addition to cleaning up the mess, I needed to talk to some of my clients. I decided to direct them to a co-worker while I take a leave of absence. It only seemed right since I've been so preoccupied. My company allows this after five years of employment. I've been there for seven and have never done it."

"That sounds good. I don't blame you one bit."

Karen smiled. "I'm glad you'll be off for a while. Have you heard anything from Mike?"

"Not yet."

"You will," Amanda assured. "It's only been one day since he started searching."

"In the meantime, we should plan Thanksgiving," Karen said.

"It will be fun to have it here," Amanda said. "Besides, I don't want to haul that wheelbarrow filled with pecans to your house!"

Jim laughed. "I know we discussed this earlier, but are you sure you want to have it here?"

"Absolutely."

"It's settled then," Karen said.

"Thanks! I'm looking forward to it."

"I'll buy everything if you make out a list," Jim offered.

"You don't need to buy everything," Amanda said.

"I insist."

Karen put her hand on Amanda's. "Let Jim and me handle the shopping, and then we can spend the day preparing the meal together."

"Okay, then. That would be just fine. I'm not fond of grocery shopping anyway, as you can probably tell by looking inside my refrigerator."

"Let's put together the list today, and Jim and I will take it with us."

Amanda nodded. "I'm assuming both of you like the traditional feast, and you have no food allergies or aversion to anything. Am I right?"

"We like everything except sweet potatoes with marshmallows," Jim said, crinkling his nose. "I mean, why would you ruin a perfectly good sweet potato?"

"I totally agree."

They made out the list with all the essentials, and the only argument they got into was over canned cranberry sauce. Amanda thought the canned stuff was disgusting and wanted to make it from fresh cranberries, while Jim said he'd always liked the canned kind the best. Since she wasn't in love with cranberry sauce anyway, Amanda acquiesced on that. The conversation was animated and jovial, and for a brief time, they seemed to have forgotten the past few days. They had no idea at the time that Mike had just uncovered a disturbing coincidence about Margarethe and Sophia.

Jim's phone vibrated on the table as they were finishing up the grocery list. "I don't recognize the number, so this could be another threat," he said warily. He answered it anyway.

It was Mike, and he sounded serious. "You might want to put me on speaker," he said.

Jim did. "Okay. You're on."

There was a pause and the sound of shuffling paper. "Okay, so I've found information on Albert Kleiner. Amanda was correct to point out that one of his descendants is Senator Bart Kleiner. I also found that Albert Kleiner had a sister named Johanna. Johanna married a man by the name of Edward Johnson. They had a son named Thomas Johnson, and I've found a record that indicates he is the same man who was married to Sophia Mueller."

Karen gasped. "Unbelievable! Thomas Johnson was the nephew of Albert Kleiner!"

"That really is strange," Jim said, shaking his head.

"It certainly is, but I don't know how it relates to what's been happening to you," Mike said, and then added, "I'm going to keep searching."

"I hate to sound like a conspiracy theorist," Amanda said hesitantly, "but there are rumors that anyone who crosses Senator Bart Kleiner ends up dead. It always appears to be an accident, but there's speculation on that."

"I've heard those rumors as well," Mike agreed. "I've also heard that Senator Kleiner is planning to run for president in the next election."

"So, what's next?" Jim asked.

"I'm going to find out if the Kleiner family is connected to Hank's beating and the break-in at your home."

"You know, I'm not a fan of Bart Kleiner, but I hope there's no connection," Amanda said.

Karen nodded. "I hope not, too."

"I don't really care if there *is* or *isn't*. I just want to know who's behind this," Jim said.

"And I'm going to make sure we find out," Mike assured. "I'll call as soon as I find more information."

"Thanks," Jim said before he clicked off the phone.

Karen said, "I have to admit, this is hard to believe."

"Ditto that," Amanda agreed. "I didn't think there would be any connection between Sophia's husband and the Kleiner family. It is quite disturbing."

"Indeed, it is," Jim said. "However, I'm looking forward to finding out the truth."

"Me, too," Karen agreed.

"Whatever it is, I know you can deal with it," Amanda assured.

"I think so, too," Karen said, and then turned to Jim. "You look like you need some rest. Do you want to head back home now?"

"What gave it away—the dark circles under my eyes or how bloodshot they appear?"

"Both."

"Okay, then. Get your stuff and let's go."

As Karen collected her bag from the bedroom, Jim turned to Amanda and whispered, "Thanks for dealing with all of this. You've been such a help to Karen, and I greatly appreciate it. She doesn't seem as anxious as she once did."

"No problem at all, but I believe she's found some inner peace on her own."

Jim nodded and was about to say something else, but Karen returned with her bag.

"Have a safe trip home," Amanda said as she walked them to the front door.

"Please set your alarm system, and make sure your doors are locked," Jim advised.

"Don't worry. I will."

Chapter 14

That night, Amanda had no dreams—at least none that she could remember the next morning. And this was perfectly fine with her, because even though she'd always liked the one about riding the horse and meeting the handsome man, she realized she didn't need the dream anymore. Jim was real, and she no longer felt alone in the world. She still missed her grandparents, but she felt as if she could count on Jim and Karen for the rest of her life. She suddenly felt the need to talk to Carolyn, so she picked up her phone and made the call.

"Well, well, well. There you are," Carolyn said when she answered. "I was just thinking of you."

"I was thinking of you, too, which is why I called. How are you?"

"My kids have been sick again—this time with an upper respiratory infection, but so far I haven't caught it. *Knock on wood.* Germs must ooze from their little fingertips."

Amanda laughed. "It does make you wonder."

"What's been going on in your world?" Carolyn asked.

Amanda was glad she wasn't pressing for information about Jim, but she knew it was coming. She decided to bring it up herself. "Remember that guy I told you I was falling for?"

"I most certainly do, but I was waiting for a report on that from you. Dish it."

"I'm still falling."

"That's it? That's all you have to say about him?"

"Yes, it is. Not enough?"

"Oh, Amanda. You disappoint me. I was hoping for details."

"No details yet. Nothing has happened, but I doubt I would share it all anyway. Goodness. We're not in high school anymore," Amanda said, snickering.

"I'll be waiting, and I'll also be waiting to meet the mystery man."

"Don't worry. You will."

"Are you happy? That's all that matters."

"Yes. I'm happier than I've been in a long time."

"Well, then, that's great news. Hey, I was going to call you today to ask if you'd like to come over for Thanksgiving."

Amanda answered quickly. "I've already made plans, but thanks for asking."

"With whom will you be dining on that day? Him?"

"Yes. *Him.*"

"So…bring him to my house."

"Not yet. Another time. Besides, I'll be with his sister, too."

Carolyn sighed in resignation. "Okay, but I'm going to hold you to it. By the way, what is the mystery man's name?"

"It's Jim."

"Does Jim have a last name?"

"I'll tell you that later."

"Argh. You're killing me, Amanda."

"I'm sorry. It's complicated."

"Isn't it always. I don't need to be worried about you, do I?"

"Not at all."

"Good. Hey, did you hear about the elderly man who was severely beaten at the cemetery in Hillsdale?"

Amanda hadn't been expecting this question, and she thought it was best not to share that she knew the intimate details. And so, she decided to play it cool for the time being. "Yes. I saw it on the news. That poor man."

"The police have no idea who did it. I just don't understand people these days."

"I don't either." Amanda thought of Officer Crenshaw, who was probably working hard to solve the case. There was an awkward silence until Carolyn spoke again.

"I should get off the phone so I can get some things done around here. You take care of yourself and have a nice Thanksgiving. I want to hear all about it, okay?"

"I'll let you know, and I hope you have a nice holiday, too."

After ending the call, Amanda felt rather guilty for keeping Carolyn in the dark about everything. However, she knew it was important to keep Jim and Karen's family situation a secret. It was approaching eleven o'clock, and she wondered if she'd hear from them. She decided it was a good time to go to the grocery store to buy snacks in case they came over later.

Amanda got home from the store a couple of hours later with a back seat filled with bags. She unloaded her car and put everything away quickly, so she could go outside with Bandy and walk through the pasture. After grabbing the house key and locking the door behind her, she ventured out at a quick pace, while the dog ran ahead. Walking had always provided an escape from the daily grind when she worked at the clinic. She was able to think and relax without interruptions because she always left her phone in the office. However, she now carried the phone whenever she walked since she was living alone in a rural area. It was merely a precaution in case she twisted her ankle or suffered a snake bite.

Amanda walked for about an hour before heading back to the house. She unlocked the door and whistled for Bandy, who came running from the pasture. As she walked into the kitchen to get a drink, her phone vibrated with an incoming call. It was Jim.

"I was wondering if I'd hear from you today," Amanda answered before he had a chance to speak.

"I'd planned to call sooner, but I've been on the phone with Mike. He has more information, as well as a plan."

"That was fast."

"It certainly was. He'd like to talk to Hank, so he'll call you soon to get the contact information."

"What's the plan?"

"Mike said that based on his research, he has reason to believe that Senator Bart Kleiner is involved. He also found out that Kleiner employs a man named Jack Simon to handle people who might be a threat to the senator's career. I'm sure you remember that Hank said he heard one of the men say that Simon would be pleased."

Amanda was stunned. "Unbelievable!"

"It certainly is. Mike wants to interview Hank, and then he wants to see if he'd be willing to go back to volunteer at the cemetery tomorrow. If he agrees, we'll meet him there. We'll go into the office to ask questions about the Mueller family, just like we did before. Mike thinks we're being watched by the goons and this will bring them out again."

Amanda wasn't sure she liked the plan. She was afraid they'd all be in danger. "So, what happens if it does bring them out again? Will we all be killed this time?"

"Mike is going to work with the police department, and we'll be watched by them as well. If anyone tries anything, they will be arrested and questioned."

Amanda sighed. "I suppose that could work, but what if it doesn't bring them out?"

"Mike has evidence they're watching us. He staked out my house last night, and he saw a dark-blue sedan with tinted windows drive by a couple of times. He also saw a couple of big bald men walking around the neighborhood after dark. I doubt it's a coincidence."

"Wow. Has he seen the car today?"

"He saw it drive by once this morning, but he thinks the men will probably be hanging out near the cemetery. My guess is they know Hank is out of the hospital, and they might be waiting for us to go talk to him again."

"Hmm. I don't understand why they would return to the scene of the crime."

"Amanda," Jim said thoughtfully, "these people are so connected that they probably think there will be no consequences for their actions. They have no fear. They're trying to intimidate us—perhaps toying with us like a cat batting around a ball of catnip. It's fun for them. Just my opinion. I could be wrong, of course."

Amanda's phone buzzed with an incoming call. Seeing it was Mike, she said, "I'll get back to you in a minute."

"No problem," Jim said quickly before disconnecting.

"Hi, Mike," Amanda answered.

"How are you?"

"Doing fine. I just got off the phone with Jim. He said you'd be calling for Hank's contact information."

"Yes, I'd like to ask him a few questions. I'd also like to find out if he'd be willing to go to the cemetery office tomorrow, so Jim and Karen can return to inquire about their family. This might lure the two men back there. I've spoken to Officer Crenshaw, and he'll also be there ready to arrest them."

"I definitely want to see these men caught and put in jail."

"I'm fairly certain they'll show up," Mike said. "Anyway, I hope they will. I haven't spoken to the FBI yet, but I plan to do so if we catch them. I sincerely suspect that Senator Bart Kleiner is involved."

"I have the same feeling," Amanda agreed. "Hold on a minute. I'll get Hank's information for you."

"Thanks."

She gave him Hank's number, and then said, "Good luck. I'll wait to hear from you."

"I'll call you back with the details. Talk to you soon."

Amanda then called Jim, who answered right away. "That didn't take long," he said.

"Mike got straight to the point."

"Do you think Hank will go for it?"

"Hard to say, but he wouldn't have given me his phone number and address if he never wanted to hear from us again. He also seemed eager to help when we last spoke."

"So, we'll just wait to hear from Mike at this point."

"Yes, and I think it will be soon since he wants to do this tomorrow."

"Probably because he spotted the goons, and he knows he needs to strike fast before they leave."

"I still don't get it," Amanda said.

"Me neither, but I'll bet we'll have some answers soon."

"How's Karen doing?"

Jim sighed and hesitated before answering. "She seems to be okay. She just wants to catch these guys."

"Good. All right, then. We'll wait for Mike to call with the specifics...if Hank agrees to the plan."

"I don't know what we'll do if he doesn't, but I'm sure Mike will figure something out. He appears to be very good at his job," Jim said.

"I was always impressed with him whenever he came into the clinic. Never thought I'd need him though."

"And I certainly had no idea I'd ever need a PI."

Amanda then decided to get off the phone so she could clean her house. She also needed to burn off some nervous energy, however, she kept the nervous part to herself. "I'd better go now. I need to do some work around here in case the next few days are busy."

"Okay. You have fun with that, and I'll wait for Mike's call."

They broke the connection, and Amanda pulled out the vacuum. For some reason, she did her best thinking while sucking up dust bunnies. She smiled at the thought of the word. Her grandmother always said she was hunting dust bunnies while she vacuumed. As a child, Amanda thought there were bunnies hiding in various places throughout the house. Even when she figured out what they really were, she still played along. By then, it had become a fun game with her grandmother pretending like she'd spotted a creature in one of the rooms. She'd shout for Amanda to come, and just before she got there, the bunny always escaped. On this day, though, Amanda vacuumed the entire house while deep in thought about what might bring an old vendetta into the present day. She also dusted, cleaned bathrooms, and washed sheets. And afterward, she barely remembered the process. The chores seemed so mundane in comparison to the mystery of Margarethe.

As evening approached, she was beginning to wonder if Hank had agreed to Mike's plan, and she hoped she'd hear an answer by the end of the day. There had to be a plan by then anyway if they were going to meet at the cemetery the next day. She turned on the TV to search for a comedy movie, and it was then that Mike called.

"Hello," she answered quickly.

"Sorry, it's taken so long to get back to you. I received Hank's approval, and then I called Jim to give him the final details. We just got off the phone."

She was partially relieved and a bit nervous at the same time. "That's good. So, what's the plan?"

"Hank will arrive at the cemetery at nine o'clock in the morning. That was the usual time he came into work, so I thought it would be best that he appeared to be on the same schedule. You, Jim, and Karen will arrive at around noon—that is, if you want to go with them. However, I don't think your presence is mandatory, since you aren't part of the family. There will be an undercover police officer watching Jim and Karen's house while they're gone. Officer Crenshaw and I will be watching the cemetery, and there will be another officer nearby. Jim will carry a notebook to give the illusion that he plans to write down family information. You'll all enter the office, and then Jim will ask Hank a question about the Mueller family. He will specifically inquire about his great-grandfather Johann. Hank will do a search on the computer, just as he did before. You'll stick around inside for twenty minutes, and then walk over to Johann's grave."

"What if the guys don't come? Will we need to come back the next day?"

"Yes, you'll return the next day. However, I have a hunch the two men will show up tomorrow. I've had Jim and Karen's house under surveillance, and I've seen them lurking around. I took photos of their car—which is a Cadillac, by the way. I also followed them to the local convenience store, where they used the bathroom and picked up snacks. I can't get the license number though, because there's a dark tinted piece of plastic covering the plate."

"Oh, my. I hope they haven't been near my house."

"I believe they are only focused on the Dorions."

"That makes sense if this is truly about the Mueller family."

"We'll know soon enough. Anyway—about tomorrow. If you choose to go, then I think you should drive to Jim and Karen's house instead of them coming to get you. Arrive there at eleven o'clock to allow for plenty of time to get to the cemetery by noon. And one more thing—Hank will be wired, so we can hear what's going on in there. Good luck, and we'll talk when this is over."

"I think I need to be there, so I'll plan to go. Thanks for the information," Amanda said before clicking off the phone. She then called Jim.

"Hi, Amanda," he answered.

"Hey, I just got off the phone with Mike, and he told me about tomorrow's plan. I'll be at your house at eleven o'clock."

"Looking forward to it," Jim joked. "Actually, I'm not. Anything could go wrong."

"I know. I have some trepidation myself, but this needs to play out."

Jim sighed. "And so, it will."

Amanda changed the subject. "Is Karen okay with the plan?"

"Surprisingly, she's energized by it. She wants to get closure."

"That's a good attitude to have. I'll see you tomorrow, and please give Karen my best."

"Will do."

Amanda spent the rest of the evening trying to relax so she could get to sleep, but nothing worked. She even drank a glass of red wine, which seemed to energize her even more. She checked the front and back doors to make sure they were locked, and then checked the alarm system. She also shut the curtains in case anyone was lurking outside. For the first time since moving back home, she was rather anxious about living on the outskirts of town where no one would hear her if she screamed.

It took a couple of hours for Amanda to fall asleep, and she woke up several times after that. When her alarm went off at seven o'clock in the morning, she cursed out loud, and then got out of bed and opened the shades. It was a cold and rainy Friday morning—setting the mood for the trip to the cemetery. She decided to make the best of the morning before she had to leave, so she drank an entire pot of coffee, responded to emails, and took a walk with Bandy. She then made a quick bite to eat before getting ready to go to Jim and Karen's. She chose to wear jeans and a purple sweater, along with her most comfortable shoes—a pair of black suede lace-up flats—not attractive by any means, but she didn't care. She wanted to be able to make a quick exit if she had to do so.

Amanda's Volvo handled well on wet roads, but she drove a bit slower since it was cold enough to create a thin layer of ice. She arrived at the Dorions' home ten minutes later than Mike had requested, but there was plenty of time to arrive at the cemetery by noon. Jim answered the door looking determined and bold in a black leather jacket and dark-colored jeans. "Are you ready?" he asked.

"Yes. I suppose so," Amanda said, letting out a heavy sigh.

Karen stood behind Jim, and she appeared to be exhausted with dark circles under her eyes. She was wearing a pair of faded jeans and a pale gray sweater, which gave Amanda the impression that she wanted to disappear.

"Did you sleep okay?" Amanda asked.

Karen shook her head and frowned. "I had a nightmare last night."

"I'm sorry to hear that. Maybe you're just nervous about today," Amanda assured.

"I'm a bit scared, but I'm also ready to do this."

"We'll be okay," Jim said confidently. He looked at his watch. "We should get going though."

Chapter 15

They climbed into Jim's Subaru—Karen got into the back seat, and Amanda sat in the front. Jim was quiet and appeared to be deep in thought. Amanda watched him take several glances at the rearview mirror in case they were being followed out of the neighborhood. They weren't. However, as they got closer to the highway, she noticed a dark-blue Cadillac with tinted windows parked on a side street. There was no mistaking it. It was the same car they'd seen parked by the side of the road on the day Hank was beaten. She looked at Jim, and he nodded. Neither of them said anything to Karen, who had fallen asleep. There was no reason to scare her. The windshield wipers made a rhythmic whishing sound, which helped Amanda relax a bit. They didn't see the Cadillac on the highway. The driver must have hung back so he wouldn't be noticed.

As they pulled into the gravel parking lot of the cemetery, there was still no sign of the car, and she breathed a sigh of relief. Hank's white Honda Civic was parked in its usual spot, so everything was going according to Mike's plan.

"We're here," Jim announced loudly, turning toward his sister in the back seat.

Karen awoke, yawning. "Already?"

"Sorry, Sis, but we have a mystery to solve."

"Okay, then. Did you remember to bring the notebook, so you can act like you're writing down family information?"

"It's in the door panel by my seat," Jim answered, pulling out a black spiral.

A silence fell among them for a few seconds before Amanda spoke. "We should go. From what Mike told me, we need to be inside for twenty minutes, and then we need to go to Johann Mueller's grave."

Karen got out of the car first, and Amanda and Jim followed. No one carried an umbrella, so they were wet from the falling drizzle by the time they walked inside the office. Hank stood behind the counter looking very determined. His arm was no longer in a sling, but his eyes were still bruised from his broken nose. Although he put on a good act of being brave, Amanda noticed his right hand was slightly trembling.

"Hello! What brings you in here on such a yucky day?" he asked.

"We have a few more questions about the Mueller family if you have time," Jim answered calmly.

"I have all the time in the world. What can I do for you?"

"We'd like to find out more about our great-grandfather Johann," Karen answered.

It was then that the door to the office opened, and two bald men stepped inside. They looked as if they could be identical twin brothers, except one had blue eyes and the other had brown eyes. And Hank had been right. They were big. In fact, Amanda estimated that they were well over six feet tall. They were each wearing a black trench coat, and the blue-eyed guy had his hand inside his right pocket. Amanda noticed the pocket was bulging, and she knew there was probably a gun inside. "What's going on in here?" the man asked. He then pulled out a pistol.

Karen gasped.

Jim answered. "We're doing family research." There was no waiver in his voice. In fact, he sounded angry.

Both men then looked at Hank. The one without the gun walked closer to the counter where he stood.

"I thought we took care of you last time, old man," he snarled.

Hank's hand was still trembling, but his demeanor was direct and calm. Perhaps it was because he knew there were officers nearby. "Looks like it didn't work," he said loudly.

Instead of hitting Hank, the man walked away and stood by his gun-wielding partner, who had moved dangerously close to Karen. Her mouth was open, and she appeared to be trying to scream, but she had no voice at all. Sensing fear, the man with the gun grabbed her by her hair and pointed his weapon to her head. And that's when Jim charged at him. It was also then that he shot Jim in the shoulder—no doubt, aiming for his chest. Jim still wasn't deterred as blood began to pour from the wound. He lunged at the man again. Officer Crenshaw burst through the door at that instant, and the man foolishly aimed the gun at him. Crenshaw was faster. He fired his weapon and shot him in the chest. As he fell to the floor, Karen fainted. The other goon tried to grab Hank, but another officer ran inside and got to him first. The officer quickly handcuffed him and escorted him to a waiting police cruiser. Mike was next on the scene, and then there were more police officers, as well as paramedics coming in to care for the wounded. Jim's shoulder was bleeding profusely, and they rushed him off in an ambulance. The man that Officer Crenshaw shot was seriously injured but still alive, so he was handcuffed to a gurney and transported to the hospital under another officer's supervision. Karen was stretched out on the floor, still unconscious, but a paramedic was with her. Amanda didn't know where to turn. Her heart raced as she found Hank, who was standing by the counter and doing just fine. He told the paramedics to leave him and tend to the others. Amanda had no words as she embraced him. He gently pushed her away and told her everything was going to be okay. It was then that the first tear ran down her face. The reality of the situation was beginning to soak in, and she was petrified.

"It's going to be okay," Hank repeated in a stern voice, as if he were trying to convince himself of that. His jaw appeared to be tight, and his right hand was still a bit shaky. However, he was surprisingly stoic, given the scene that lay before them. She hurried over toward Karen, who was now conscious and talking to two paramedics while she was being placed on a gurney. "My brother has been shot," Karen whispered, and then she began to sob uncontrollably.

"I'm so sorry," Amanda said tearfully. She was at a loss for words, and there was nothing she could say that would help.

One of the paramedics turned to Amanda and said, "We're taking her to the hospital to get checked out. You can ride along if you want."

"I'll do that," she responded as she walked beside the gurney toward the waiting ambulance. It was still raining, which added to the gloom.

Officer Crenshaw ran to catch up to Amanda before the ambulance doors were shut. "I'm sorry, but I really need you to stay here to answer some questions," he said breathlessly.

She didn't argue, but she wasn't happy about sending Karen to the hospital without anyone with her. "It's okay," Karen whispered. "Come when you can."

Amanda stroked her hand and nodded before stepping out of the ambulance to join Crenshaw.

Mike and Hank were waiting for them in the office when they got there. Hank was seated in a chair behind the counter, and Crenshaw asked Amanda if she'd like to sit down, too. She did.

"We had audio and were able to hear most of what went on when the two men came inside, but we don't have video. I'd like for both of you to provide a statement in case we missed something," Crenshaw explained.

Hank gave his account first, and then Amanda added some of the details he missed. After Crenshaw was satisfied with the report, he told them they were free to go. Since Amanda hadn't driven her car to the cemetery, Hank took her to the hospital to check on Jim and Karen.

"I'm getting tired of coming to this place," Hank said as they walked through the entrance.

Amanda couldn't think of an appropriate response, so she merely nodded. Hank then pointed to a silver-haired lady standing at the information counter, who appeared to be quite upset. "That's my friend, Debbie Blake," he said.

Debbie was talking loudly, frantically asking if anyone named Hank Autin had been admitted. The man behind the counter was shaking his head.

"Are you sure?" Debbie asked. "Could he have been admitted to another hospital?"

"I'm here!" Hank shouted.

Debbie turned and exclaimed, "Thank goodness! I heard the sirens going toward the cemetery. I drove over there, but the police wouldn't allow me inside. I didn't know what to do, so I came to the hospital to see if you might be here. What in the world happened?"

"I'm okay," Hank assured. He gave her a brief rundown of the situation, and then said, "We need to go check on a couple of folks before I come back to your house."

"I knew you shouldn't have gone to the cemetery," Debbie said angrily.

Hank shook his head. "I had to. It was part of the plan to catch the guys who beat me up, and it worked."

Debbie didn't look entirely convinced, but she nodded and said, "I'm just glad you weren't hurt."

"Thank you. Unfortunately, one of the good guys *has* been hurt and a nice lady collapsed, so we need to check on them."

"I understand. I'll wait here, and I hope they're okay," Debbie said, looking at Amanda. "I'm sorry. I didn't mean to be rude. Hank is a good friend, and I was so scared he was hurt again."

"I understand completely. I'm Amanda. We'll talk later," she said quickly, walking toward the hall.

"Wait," Hank called. "We need to get a room number."

The man behind the counter provided Karen's room number but said that Jim had been transported to a hospital in Overland Park. Amanda ran down the hall to the room, where she found Karen, but she was asleep. A nurse came in shortly afterward and said that Karen's heart rate was too fast when she arrived, so they needed to monitor it for a few hours. This left Amanda with a decision to make. She didn't want to leave Karen, but she knew that depending on Jim's condition, she might need to go to Overland Park. A call to patient information verified that he was in surgery. Amanda decided it would be best to go there and wait.

"I'm going to order a ride and go see Jim," she said.

"Why don't I just drive you to get your car," Hank offered.

"Thank you, but it's at Jim's house," Amanda muttered. She suddenly felt exasperated. Hank must have picked up on it.

"It's okay," he said gently. "I don't mind at all."

"Thanks. I just thought of something though. I don't want Karen to wake up alone, so I'm wondering if you could stay in her room. I don't mind paying for a ride."

"I'd be happy to stay with her," Hank said. "I just don't want you to be alone either."

Debbie Blake was standing at the entrance waiting for them, and he told her about the plan. She looked at Amanda and said, "I can drive you to the hospital in Overland Park. You've been through so much, and I think it would be best if you were with someone."

Amanda didn't want to impose, but she was relieved Debbie could drive her. "Thank you so much."

"I'll go back to Karen's room and wait," Hank said. "I hope Jim is okay."

"Let's hope for the best," Amanda said.

Debbie walked swiftly to her black Toyota Camry, and Amanda followed closely behind.

"Oh, no," Amanda said, as she got inside the vehicle. "I need to feed my dog and let her outside."

"We can do that," Debbie said. "Where do you live?"

"Just a few miles south of the hospital. I'm sorry."

"It's no problem at all."

As soon as the car came to a stop in the driveway, Amanda jumped out and ran toward the house. Bandy was pacing impatiently by the door. After a quick romp outside, she came inside to eat, and the women were back on the road.

Debbie let Amanda off at the hospital entrance, and then went to park the car. When Amanda checked in at the front desk, she found that Jim was out of surgery and in recovery. However, because she wasn't family, the staff couldn't provide much information. She sat impatiently in the waiting room, hoping he would be allowed to have visitors soon. Debbie sat beside her, and Amanda was grateful for her presence. She noticed for the first time that Debbie had beautiful green eyes and prominent cheekbones. Her silver hair was cut into a bob with feathery bangs that covered her eyebrows.

"Thank you," Amanda said. "You have no idea how much I appreciate this."

Debbie stroked her hand. "I'm glad I'm here with you."

They talked for nearly two hours, and then a nurse announced that Jim could have a visitor. Debbie stayed in the waiting room, and Amanda followed the nurse down the hall. Jim was awake but groggy. He recognized Amanda though. "Hi," he whispered. "I'm glad you're okay."

"I'm physically just fine, but I've been extremely worried about you," Amanda said, walking closer to the bed. Jim's chest and left arm and shoulder were covered with bandages, and there was an IV attached to the top of his right hand.

"They tell me I'm going to live. How's my sister?"

"She's fine, but she's in the hospital in Paola for observation. Her heart rate was too high when the ambulance brought her there."

"She's had that before. She gets tachycardia if she becomes too upset."

"Understandable in this situation. I'm glad she's at the hospital. She was sleeping when I left. I didn't want her to wake up alone, so Hank is staying with her while I'm here."

"What about that jerk who shot me? Where is he?"

"He was taken to a hospital, but I don't know anything else about him."

A nurse came into the room and said it was time to leave, so Amanda excused herself. "I'll come back tomorrow," she called, walking out the door.

Debbie stood up as Amanda entered the waiting room. "How is he?"

"He's a bit groggy, but he was able to talk to me. I'm relieved beyond belief that he's okay."

"So glad to hear that. Hank and I have been texting, and he said that Karen is awake and alert. She's worried about Jim. I'll text Hank and let him know so he can tell her."

"Thank you again."

"You need to go home and get some rest. I'm sure you're exhausted," Debbie said as they walked to her car.

"I need to check on Karen. I won't be able to sleep until I see her."

"We can do that," Debbie said. "By the way, Karen is being discharged soon. Hank would like to bring her to my house because she doesn't want to go home. You can come, too, if you'd like."

"Thank you. I really appreciate it, but I need to go home to take care of my dog—and if it's okay with you, I might have Karen stay with me tonight. However, I really should pick up my car."

"Okay, but don't worry about your car. You won't need it tonight, and I don't think you should be driving after the day you've had. Hank and I will pick you up tomorrow and take you to get it. What do you say?"

"Thank you, Debbie. I'm so tired right now that going home sounds wonderful—even without my vehicle."

"It's settled then. Let's go get Karen, so both of you can get some sleep."

Chapter 16

Hank met them at the entrance when they arrived at the hospital. "She's doing fine," he said as they walked to Karen's room. She still looked pale, but Amanda was pleased that she seemed to be alert and was sitting in a chair.

"How's Jim?" Karen asked.

"He's going to be okay," Amanda answered, and then asked, "Are you feeling better?"

"I guess. My heart rate is back to normal, so they are releasing me. I'm supposed to see a cardiologist for an additional checkup as soon as I can get an appointment."

"That would be a wise thing to do. Would you like to spend the night at my house?"

"Absolutely."

Amanda nodded toward Debbie. "This is Hank's friend, Debbie Blake. She'll drive us there, and then return tomorrow to take us to pick up my car."

Debbie extended her hand to Karen. "It's nice to meet you."

"Nice to meet you, too. Thanks for doing this."

"It's no problem."

Karen stood up. "I've already signed the discharge papers, so I can go now."

"Great," Amanda said. "Let's get out of here."

A nurse rushed into the room pushing an empty wheelchair. "Please have a seat, Ms. Dorion, and I'll take you to the car."

"I can walk."

The nurse shook her head. "It's hospital policy."

"Okay," Karen surrendered, and then carefully sat down.

"I'll pull my car around to the entrance and meet you there," Debbie called, walking out of the room.

Amanda and Hank followed. The nurse released the brakes on the wheelchair and pushed Karen down the hall.

Hank put his arm around Debbie before she went outside and said, "Thanks. I'll meet you back at your place."

"Sure thing," Debbie said, and then walked swiftly toward the parking lot.

The nurse helped Karen into the front seat of the car, and Amanda got into the back seat, and they were on their way. Bandy was waiting by the door and barked as the two women entered the house. Amanda gave her a treat before letting her outside. She then turned to Karen. "You can get something to eat if you'd like. I'm going to take a shower first."

"Thanks, but I'm not hungry at all. I think I'll take a shower, too, and then go to bed."

"I understand," Amanda said. She poured a glass of water and went to her bedroom. *This was one day that needed to end*, she thought.

The next morning came too quickly. It was Saturday—only five more days until Thanksgiving. Amanda wondered if Jim would be out of the hospital by then. Her body felt sore from the stress of the day before, and she didn't want to leave her bed. Of course, Bandy let her know it was time to eat and go outside, so she shuffled into the kitchen and prepared her food. The dog gobbled the kibble as if she hadn't eaten in a year, and Amanda rushed her out the door. Yawning, she then made coffee. Karen wasn't up yet, so she moved around quietly to allow her to sleep longer.

When Amanda turned on the morning news and saw the local report, she nearly spewed coffee out of her mouth. The shooting at the cemetery was the lead story, and a mugshot of one of the men was featured. The other man had died on the way to the hospital after being shot by Officer Crenshaw. The news anchor announced that one person was still in the hospital in stable condition, and Amanda was glad there was no mention that it was Jim. There was footage of Amanda walking with Hank to the cemetery parking lot as they were leaving to go to the hospital. She hadn't even noticed the media being there at the time. Hank's name was reported, probably because he'd been recently featured in the news after he was beaten up at the cemetery. The news anchor also stated that the shooting might have been related to that incident. Even though Amanda's name wasn't reported, her face was clearly visible in the footage. She knew that most of the people in town, in addition to her former co-workers in Kansas City, would have seen the clip by now. She suspected her phone was now filled with texts. She was afraid to look at it, but she did, and it was indeed filled. In fact, her voicemail also had so many messages that she was certain no other calls could come through. Carolyn had called and texted multiple times. Amanda knew she needed to respond, but she wanted to check on Jim first. He answered his mobile on the first ring.

"Good morning," he said. His voice was much stronger than the day before.

"You sound better."

"Not quite, but I'm getting there. How's Karen?"

"Shaken up, but she came home with me and went right to bed. She's still asleep or I'd put her on the phone to talk to you."

"That's okay. Let her sleep. I watched the news this morning and saw the report about the cemetery. I'm glad they didn't say my name. I'd have dozens of texts if they had."

"Tell me about it," Amanda said. "My phone is full since the media showed the video of me."

"Yes. I saw that, too. I also saw that the man who shot me died on the way to the hospital. I hope the police can obtain information from the other guy as to why they did this."

"Me, too. This shouldn't have happened."

"I'm sorry you got caught up in this."

"I could have stayed home yesterday, but I wanted to be there. Granted, I didn't know there would be a shooting, but…"

"I know, but I'm still sorry, Amanda. This is more than you signed up for when you agreed to take my sister as a client."

"She's no longer my client, remember? I went there as a friend, and I don't regret that."

"Thank you. Hey, the doctor is coming in, so I need to go. I'm sure it's to tell me when I can go home."

"Okay, I'll talk to you later," Amanda said, and then ended the connection. She knew it was time to call Carolyn.

She'd never heard Carolyn sound upset before, until she answered the phone. Her voice was high-pitched— nearly screaming.

"There you are! I've been worried sick! Do you know how scary it is to see your friend on TV after a shooting? Do you?" she shrieked.

Amanda breathed deeply. "Calm down. I'm okay."

"What were you doing there anyway?" Carolyn asked, her voice still at a shrill pitch.

Amanda knew she couldn't provide details yet, so she answered as best as she could. "I was helping a couple of friends with genealogy research. Two men burst through the door and shot one of my friends."

"Was this friend the guy you told me about? Jim was his name, I believe. And why on earth would anyone shoot someone for doing genealogy research?"

"Yes. It was Jim. He's in the hospital, and he's going to be okay. His sister was there, too, and she's staying with me. She was extremely upset. I haven't been able to call you until now, and I'm sorry."

"Is this Jim guy trouble or something? I don't understand why someone would burst into a cemetery office and shoot him."

"No, he's not trouble. He's a wonderful person, and we don't know why this happened. The police will get to the bottom of it though. I'm certain of that."

Carolyn sighed and paused. "Amanda, you might be too trusting. I think you should make sure there's nothing else going on here. I'm worried about you."

"I'm fine. I assure you, although, today I'm very tired."

"Okay, but please know I'm here if you need to talk about this. I care about you, Amanda. We've been friends forever, so please don't block me out."

"I know that, and I'm not blocking you out. I'm letting the police do the investigation, and I don't want to speculate. The important thing is that Jim is all right and his sister is, too. I should probably get off the phone now though, because she might be waking up soon. I'd like to make breakfast for her."

"Okay. Keep me posted and take care of yourself, my friend," Carolyn said, her voice still at an octave higher than usual.

"Will do," Amanda said as she clicked off the call. She wasn't thrilled with the prospect of returning the other messages, so she decided to send an email to everyone who called or texted to let them know she was okay but didn't feel like talking. Instead of making breakfast for Karen, she went to her computer and did just that.

Karen came into the office as Amanda sent the last email. She'd already showered and dressed and looked surprisingly well.

"You look great," Amanda said. "Did you sleep okay?"

"I really did."

"I was going to make breakfast for you, but I decided to respond to my messages first."

"You don't need to do that. I'll just make myself something, and I'll pay you for groceries, too. I've been here eating your food a lot lately."

"You'll do no such thing. I'm happy to have you here."

"That's very kind of you," Karen said. "I don't know if you've talked to Jim today, but he texted me a few minutes ago. He's doing fine, which is such a relief. The doctor said he can come home tomorrow."

Amanda grinned. "That's great! I talked to him earlier, but he had to get off the phone because the doctor was coming into his room. I'll go take a shower now while you eat, and then I'll call Debbie Blake. After she takes us to my car, we can drop by to see Jim."

"That sounds good. I probably need to pick up his car from the cemetery, too."

"We can do that as well."

Debbie arrived about thirty minutes after Amanda's call. She brought Hank with her, who seemed happy to ride along. It was cold and cloudy outside, but everyone was grateful the rain had ended. They talked about the day before and attempted to make sense out of what happened. No one could think of any reason why someone would be concerned about a family's genealogy project. They arrived at Jim and Karen's house with no new ideas, but Amanda was hopeful that Mike would get to the bottom of it. The house appeared to be fine with no sign of a break-in, so Hank and Debbie left. Amanda warmed up her car, and she and Karen went to the hospital to see Jim. He was sleeping when they arrived, so they sat in the chairs next to his bed and didn't make any noise. It didn't take long before Jim sensed their presence, and he awoke with a grin. Amanda was happy to see the twinkle back in his eyes. Karen quickly went to his bedside and hugged him, careful not to touch his bandages.

"I was afraid you were gone," she said tearfully.

"No such luck, Sis," he said. "You're stuck with me."

"And for that, I am glad."

Jim looked at Amanda still seated in the chair. "You can come over here, too."

She went to his bedside and leaned toward him. "It's so good to see that you're doing better."

"I'm told I can get out of here tomorrow."

"That's what I heard."

Karen interrupted. "Your car is still at the cemetery, but I'm going to drive it back home today. I have the spare set of keys, so don't worry about trying to locate yours right now."

"Thanks," Jim said. "Have you been by the house yet?"

"Yes. We needed to get Amanda's car, and everything appears to be fine."

Jim again grinned. "Good, and I assume that Mister Turtle is running okay?"

"Now, Jim," Amanda said, smiling. "You know that turtles don't run."

He snickered, and Karen rolled her eyes.

The nurse came in with lunch, but Jim indicated he wasn't hungry.

"You need to eat," Karen said.

"I'm not hungry, and the food is terrible here."

Amanda eyed the chocolate pudding cup on the tray. "At least eat your pudding. You need something in your stomach."

Jim nodded. "I think I can do that, but I need a bit of help opening it."

Amanda peeled the top off the cup, and then sat down so he could eat. "I've been thinking about Thanksgiving," she said hesitantly. "We've recently met some people who have helped us during this strange situation. I think we should invite Hank, Debbie, Mike, and Phillip to join us for dinner at my house. Mike and Phillip's families would also be invited, of course."

Karen was quick to respond. "That's a wonderful idea!"

"I agree," Jim said.

Amanda was happy to hear it. "Good."

They talked a little while longer until Jim's eyes grew heavy. Amanda knew he was probably still on medication from the surgery. Karen hugged her brother one last time before they left to pick up his car.

As they got closer to the cemetery, Amanda observed each car they passed. She knew the dark-blue sedan had been taken away, but she was still on alert. As luck would have it, there was nothing out of the ordinary, and Jim's car was parked exactly where they had left it. She didn't know what she was expecting could have happened to it. It was certainly safe with the heavy police presence during the past couple of days.

Karen pulled the spare set of keys from her purse. "Thanks for having me over last night," she said before getting out of the car.

Amanda wasn't sure if Karen should go home alone, so she asked, "Do you want to stay again tonight?"

"I should probably go home. It's closer to the hospital, and I need to pick up Jim tomorrow."

"I understand. Let me know if you need any help," Amanda said. She didn't want to be pushy.

Karen's eyes filled with tears. "I'll let you know. And I want to thank you for everything you've done."

"No thanks needed," Amanda said softly. She watched Karen get into the car, waited until it started okay, and then drove away.

She came home to a feisty dog, who wanted food and time to romp outside, as usual. After tending to Bandy's needs, she decided to check her emails. They had piled up, as people had replied to her morning message. Amanda sighed and then responded to each email. She was glad people cared, but she felt rather drained. After she was done, she realized she hadn't eaten since breakfast, so she cooked some rice and vegetables. She then decided to turn on the news but quickly regretted it. Reporters were trying to speculate on what might have been the motive for the shooting, and their ideas were far-fetched. Amanda didn't want to hear it, so she turned off the TV. She thought about when she first moved from the city and how excited she was to get away from stress. And now, she realized there was no escaping it, no matter where she went to hide. That is exactly what she'd been doing— hiding. *Even turtles had to eventually pop their heads out from their shells,* she thought. For this evening, however, Amanda decided to go to bed and look at travel magazines. She had always promised herself she'd take a cruise but had never done it. *Perhaps*, she thought, *it was time to get serious about that*.

She awoke the next morning feeling much better. *It was amazing what sleep can do for a person,* she thought. Bandy was waiting by the back door, so Amanda followed her outside on the deck. The air was cold, but the rising sun was welcoming. She stood briefly and breathed in the freshness of the morning before she brought the dog back inside to feed her. The mundane routine to which she was accustomed was comforting after what she'd witnessed at the cemetery. She started the coffee pot and made a bowl of cereal. The earthy aroma of coffee soon spread throughout the kitchen. Amanda had never grown tired of that scent, and on this day, it smelled even better. As she sat down to enjoy the first cup, her phone vibrated. It was Karen.

"Good morning," Amanda answered.

"How are you doing?" Karen asked.

"I'm rested and ready to take on the day. How about you?"

"The same. I didn't have any nightmares either. That's always a good thing."

"Yes, it is, but I have a feeling your dreams won't be bothering you any longer. You've survived a scary ordeal, and you've come through it just fine. That will provide you with confidence in knowing you can handle anything."

"I believe you, Amanda," Karen said, and then changed the subject. "I need to tell you that Mike left a phone message saying he wants to have a conference call with us at two o'clock this afternoon. I'm going to pick up Jim within the hour. Do you want to meet us at our house before the call?"

"Thanks. I wouldn't miss it. I wonder if he has any news."

"Me, too. We'll know soon enough though. I'll see you later."

"I'll be there," Amanda said.

Chapter 17

When she arrived that afternoon, Karen came to the
door looking radiant in a bronze-colored sweater. Jim
was lounging on the couch. His arm was in a sling, but
Amanda was relieved that he looked strong and alert.
He smiled when he saw her, and she felt her body grow
warm.

"Hello," Amanda said. "You look great!"

"Thanks. I'm feeling much better," Jim responded.

"I can't wait to hear from Mike. This is going to be
interesting."

"I have a feeling it might," Jim agreed. He looked at
his phone to check the time. "Only three more minutes
until he calls."

"In that case," Karen said, "I'm running to the
bathroom first."

Jim's phone rang before she returned. After scanning
the caller's number, he said, "It's Mike." He then
handed the phone to Amanda. "Since I only have one
available hand—you can answer it."

"Hello, this is Amanda."

"I'm sorry," Mike said. "I thought I was calling
Jim."

"You did, but he asked me to answer since his arm is
in a sling."

"Ah, I understand. Would you like to put the phone
on speaker?"

"Sure," Amanda said, pressing the button. Karen
came back and sat down on the floor next to the couch,
and Amanda decided to do the same.

"Okay, is everyone here?" Mike asked.

"Yes," they all said in unison.

"I have some news to share." He paused. "Some very interesting news."

"Go on," Amanda prodded.

Mike took a deep breath and said, "First of all, I'm sure you've heard that one of the men died on the way to the hospital. His name was Brent Turnbell. The living man's name is Conrad McCoy, and he has been questioned extensively. He has confessed to being hired to harass and threaten anyone digging into information about the Mueller family. He said that he and Brent were working for Jack Simon. I had already discovered that Simon is employed by Senator Bart Kleiner to handle people who might be a threat to his career. Simon obviously hired the two goons to assist him in this situation. Kleiner and Simon have also been spotted playing golf together in recent days. As it turns out, the FBI has been watching Simon for a while, due to his possible link to a couple of missing persons. Because of this, the FBI is now involved with the case. They have now arrested and questioned Simon, and he is also the person who broke into Jim and Karen's home. That way, Conrad McCoy and Brent Turnbell were free to beat up Hank."

"Unbelievable," Amanda interrupted. Jim and Karen looked at each other, shaking their heads.

"That's not all," Mike continued. "Simon's interrogation has revealed other disturbing things. He was responsible for the deaths of two people— deaths that were originally deemed accidental. He admitted that he was hired by Senator Bart Kleiner to kill them. It is likely that there are others currently listed as missing persons, who were also murdered by Simon by order of the senator, but that hasn't been proven yet. In addition, Kleiner hired Simon to make sure no one found out about his family's past involvement with the Mueller family. According to Simon, Kleiner admitted to him that his family was responsible for killing Margarethe and her daughter, Sophia. His ancestor, Albert Kleiner, pushed Margarethe over a river bluff in Alton, Illinois, to get back at her father over a land dispute. He was also, at one time, quite smitten with Margarethe. She'd made it known to him that she didn't feel the same way, and he had always carried a grudge against her. After Margarethe had been dead for several years, Albert convinced his nephew, Thomas Johnson, to marry Sophia. He then paid his nephew handsomely to kill her. Since Sophia was Margarethe's daughter, this was Albert's sick way of continuing his vendetta. And since Senator Kleiner knew about his family's past, and because there have been rumors about his possible link to questionable deaths—he did not want the past to surface. Senator Kleiner plans to run for president, so he certainly didn't want any dirty laundry revealed. The past murders his family committed would have helped to solidify the rumors about his own dirty deeds—kind of like the old saying about how *the apple doesn't fall far from the tree*. Simon has cut a deal with the FBI. In return for his confession and information, he'll do less prison time."

Jim was first to speak, "This is unbelievable. I don't understand why it matters what Kleiner's ancestors did. They weren't HIM! Most people would not judge him for that. However, if this is true, he's guilty of murder-for-hire, as well as continuing an evil vendetta."

"I don't get it either!" Karen shouted.

Amanda had one nagging question on her mind. "Has Senator Kleiner been arrested?"

"Good question," Mike responded. "Yes, he has and is being questioned as we speak. His attorney is with him, though, so I'm certain he won't say much. You'll no doubt see this on the news very soon."

"Oh, my," Karen said. "I hope we don't have to testify in court."

"You might," Mike said.

Jim shook his head in disgust. "I'm afraid I won't be able to hide my anger if I take the stand."

"One thing at a time," Mike explained. "It's important to know that you're safe right now. Senator Kleiner is a bit tied up at the moment, so he won't be hiring anyone to come after you."

"Thank goodness for that!" Jim shouted.

"I second that," Karen said.

"Well, that's all the information I have right now," Mike said.

"One more thing," Karen added. "Was anything said about what might have happened to Margarethe's husband, Hans?"

"Not a thing. I'm sorry."

Karen frowned. "We might not find out what happened to him after all."

"Sadly, we might not," Jim acknowledged. "Okay, then. Mike, please send me the bill, and I'll gladly pay it as soon as possible."

"I can wait a few weeks to see if anything else transpires if you'd like."

"That would be fine. I'll pay it when I receive the statement."

Amanda changed the subject. "Mike, we were wondering if you'd like to spend Thanksgiving with us at my house. I don't know if you're married but if so, your spouse is invited as well."

"That's very kind of you, but I'm leaving town. Thanks, though."

"No problem. I hope you have a nice holiday."

"You do the same. I'll keep all of you posted if anything else turns up."

"Take care," Amanda said before ending the connection.

They sat in silence for a few seconds after the call was over, each in apparent shock by the news. And then, Amanda said, "I know this has been a strange few days, but you should both feel relieved that these people have been caught."

Jim sighed loudly. "I do."

"I'm relieved as well," Karen agreed. "It's been a wild ride though, and I'm suddenly feeling like I need a nap."

"That's understandable," Amanda said. She glanced at Jim, who was beginning to look exhausted. "You know—I think it's best that I go home now, so you can get some sleep."

"You don't have to go," Jim said. However, his eyes closed as the words slowly came out of his mouth.

"Get some rest," she said, standing up. Karen walked her to the car.

"I'll call Phillip and tell him what's happened. Do you want me to go ahead and ask him if he'd like to share the holiday with us?" Karen asked.

"Please do. I haven't called anyone yet, so you can call Hank, too, if you want. I know we talked about spending the morning cooking together that day, but I think it would be best for everyone to arrive at around three o'clock. That way, Jim can get some extra rest."

"That sounds good. Have a safe trip home."

The next day was Monday, and Amanda called Karen after she had her morning coffee. Jim was doing better, but he'd fallen asleep again after eating breakfast. Karen said that Phillip and his wife would be coming to Thanksgiving dinner, and they were quite excited about it. Hank and Debbie would also be attending.

Amanda was thrilled to hear they were coming. "We need to make out a bigger grocery list."

"They will all bring a dish to share. Phillip said he'd bring the turkey, and Hank is bringing stuffing. Debbie Blake will bring a couple of pumpkin pies. All we need are rolls, cranberry sauce, and vegetables."

"That sounds great," Amanda said. "I'll make dinner rolls and a green bean casserole. I'll also use the pecans we gathered to make a pie."

"I can't wait to try the pie. Jim and I will bring the cranberry sauce. And since he likes the canned kind and you like it fresh—we'll bring both! We'll also bring potatoes."

"Perfect. I'm really looking forward to this. It will be a special day of thanks—that's for sure."

Amanda spent most of the day on Tuesday cleaning house, shelling pecans, and decorating for the celebration. Later in the day, she decided to go to Carolyn's for a visit. Of course, she had a lot of questions, so Amanda finally told her everything. Carolyn was relieved that things were settling down but admitted she was still concerned.

On Wednesday morning, Jim called to announce an important development in the case. The Dorions' genealogy folder had been found in Senator Kleiner's home. There would be a press conference concerning the latest development at noon. Amanda was glad more evidence had been found, but she also knew that a court trial would cause Karen a lot of anxiety if she were called to testify.

On Thanksgiving morning, Amanda made the green bean casserole and baked the pecan pie and dinner rolls. She also did some final decorating touches by adding a tablecloth and a lovely fall centerpiece to the dining room table. She placed several flower arrangements throughout the house and hung a painted wooden sign that said, "Give Thanks." She also hung a wreath on the front door. The seating around the dining room table would be tight, but there was enough room for everyone. Bandy was feisty—probably sensing there would soon be visitors. By noon, she decided the dog needed to get some of the energy out of her system, so she walked with her through the pasture. It was a gray, chilly day, but Amanda didn't mind. She breathed deeply, feeling refreshed and content. Soon, she knew, the house would be filled with wonderful people. She couldn't wait to be with all of them.

After her walk, Amanda realized she'd forgotten to set out a couple of chilled bottles of white wine, so she quickly placed one on each end of the dining room table before it was time for everyone to arrive. At 3:05 p.m., Karen and Jim pulled into the driveway. She stood at the front window and watched as Jim emerged from the passenger side of the car. He was still wearing a sling, but he looked remarkably better. Karen opened the hatch and pulled out a baking dish and a tray. She was wearing an orange and turquoise cardigan with a pair of jeans. Amanda was pleased to see that she'd chosen clothing with a color palette that was less bland than she'd worn in the past. *Perhaps Karen was happier,* she thought.

Amanda opened the front door as the Dorions rang the bell. "I'm so happy you're here!" she said. Bandy barked excitedly and ran past her to greet them.

"I must say that I'm extremely glad to be here—in more ways than one," Jim said.

Karen smiled and nodded. "I couldn't agree more."

"Well, come on inside," Amanda said.

They set the food on the dining room table and walked to the kitchen, just as the doorbell rang again. Hank and Debbie had arrived. Debbie was holding two pies, and Hank was wearing an oven mitt and holding a casserole dish filled with hot stuffing. A man carrying a large metal container walked directly behind them, and Amanda assumed him to be Phillip. He resembled Jim in the face, but his hair was gray.

"Welcome!" Amanda said as Bandy again darted past her. "I'm sorry. I'm going to put the dog in my bedroom during dinner."

"You don't need to do that," Hank said, smiling.

The man carrying the metal container then said, "I don't want you to either. Hi, I'm Phillip. Just a second, and my wife should be here, too. She forgot to get something out of the car."

Just then, a sweet-faced lady with big brown eyes walked swiftly to the porch. She was carrying a beautiful fall floral arrangement. "This is my wife, Rosie," Phillip announced.

"Pleased to meet you! I'm so glad you're here."

"Thanks so much for having us," Rosie said, handing her the flowers.

"Aww, thank you," Amanda said. She then motioned them inside. "Please, everyone, come in and make yourself at home. I see you're carrying hot food, so you can set it on the table." She pointed toward the dining room. "There's a pad under the tablecloth, so don't worry about the heat from the baking dishes."

They placed the food on the table, and Amanda quickly set the floral arrangement on the decorative baker's rack which stood against the wall. "Okay, please follow me to the kitchen," she directed. "Jim and Karen are there."

"Where do you want me to set the pumpkin pies?" Debbie asked as they walked into the kitchen.

"Just set them there next to the other one," Amanda said, pointing to the counter. "Thanks so much for baking them. I love pumpkin, and I hope you don't mind, but I also baked a pecan pie."

Debbie smiled. "Not at all. In fact, pecan is really my favorite."

Amanda introduced everyone, and they greeted each other warmly. Jim and Karen were especially thrilled to meet Phillip. There was a strong family resemblance in all three of them, and they seemed to have an invisible bond that blood relatives often share.

Amanda pulled the rolls and green bean casserole out of the oven, and then asked everyone to follow her to the dining room. After the wine was poured and the water glasses were filled, she announced that she wanted to make a toast. Everyone became silent and raised their glasses. Bandy barked once to beg for food, and everyone laughed. She'd taken up residence near Amanda's chair, and her eyes were locked on every movement.

"I'd first like to thank all of you for being here," Amanda said. "This has been an interesting few weeks, and I have a new appreciation for life and friendship. My wish is for all of us to remain connected for the rest of our lives. I'm very thankful to be able to spend this day with you and for this wonderful food we are about to eat."

"Cheers to that!" everyone shouted in unison. They each clinked their glasses and took a sip of wine.

Phillip lifted the turkey platter out of its metal carrier and placed the container on a large potholder on the baker's rack. Amanda then put some turkey on her plate. She was happy it had already been sliced, because she'd forgotten to make time for that. True to

Karen's word, there were two kinds of cranberry sauce—fresh and canned. Jim smiled as he cut a slice of the canned sauce, which had kept its perfect barrel shape. Amanda noticed that Phillip also chose the same. Everyone else took a spoonful of the fresh sauce.

Phillip snickered and said, "I noticed we're the only two who like our sauce in style."

"You bet," Jim said. "I'd say it's a family trait, but my sister doesn't like it that way," he added, winking at Karen.

"I prefer mine *not* to be in solid form," she said, laughing.

The mood was jovial as they talked and ate a wonderful meal. Amanda learned that Debbie was a retired veterinarian, and she still worked at an emergency clinic when needed. Rosie was once a meteorologist, who enjoyed going to elementary schools to discuss how weather is predicted. Hank was a retired airline pilot, but his true passion was flying small planes, which he did as often as possible. Unfortunately, he was recently grounded due to his medical issues.

Amanda revealed her history as a social worker and the reason she left the field. She even admitted that she'd originally wanted to be an artist but was afraid there would be no job prospects. Everyone was supportive and compassionate.

When it was time for dessert, Amanda asked what kind of pie everyone wanted. Fortunately, most of them requested the pumpkin. She was relieved by that, since she'd only made one pecan pie. Debbie and Karen only wanted a slice of pecan, and Hank asked for both kinds. Amanda excused herself and went to the kitchen to cut the pies. Jim followed, and of course, Bandy did also.

"Thought you might need some help," Jim said.

"That would be great. Thanks."

It didn't take long for everyone to come to the kitchen to retrieve their slice—or two slices in Hank's case.

They all returned to the table, and the banter continued.

Karen took one bite of pecan pie and smiled. "Oh, Amanda. This is delicious, and I'll never forget that we went out to gather the pecans that made it."

"Thanks," Amanda responded. "That really was fun."

It was a day to remember. That's for sure, and in the end, Bandy did get a few pieces of turkey with her own dinner. Everyone chipped in to help clean up the dishes and when the evening was over, Jim said he wished to make an announcement.

"I'd like to say how much I've enjoyed today and how thankful I am we are alive and able to spend it together. I hope we can do this again!"

Everyone agreed wholeheartedly that it had been a great Thanksgiving, and Amanda was thrilled to have hosted it.

The next three days were rather quiet, but she talked on the phone to Jim and Karen each afternoon. On Monday, Jim called to say they had received their DNA test results, and they had found several people on the list of matches who were from the Mueller line.

"You might find more history from your DNA matches that you don't know about—perhaps even information about Hans," Amanda said.

"Hmm. Good point. But I think I'll wait a little while before contacting anyone. Quite frankly, I'm on information overload when it comes to family stuff."

Amanda snickered. "Waiting might be the best option in this case."

Jim then cleared his throat, and his tone turned serious. "Karen and I have been trying to think of a way to honor Margarethe and Sophia, and we have an idea. Since Margarethe's body was never recovered, we've ordered a small stone with her name engraved on it. We plan to travel to Alton, Illinois, to put it in the river. Would you like to go with us?"

"I wouldn't miss it."

Jim continued. "And since Sophia was buried without a headstone, Karen and I are having one made for her."

"That is a lovely way to honor them," Amanda said. She was deeply touched by their gesture.

"It's the least we can do."

"When are you planning to go to Illinois?"

"Margarethe's engraved stone will be done today, so we plan to go tomorrow. We'll leave early in the morning and then stay all night there. Are you free?"

"Let me look at my busy calendar," Amanda joked, and then paused for a bit. "Okay. I think I can pencil you in for tomorrow."

"Great! We'll pick you up at seven in the morning. I've made a reservation at a bed and breakfast. You and Karen can share a room."

"I'll be ready. I'm sure my friend can take care of Bandy," Amanda confirmed.

She called Carolyn, who happily agreed to come over to take care of the dog. That evening, she packed an overnight bag and took a hot bubble bath to help her sleep better. She then set her alarm and went to bed.

Chapter 18

Jim and Karen arrived at 6:57 the following morning. Karen drove Jim's SUV, since his arm was still in the sling. The sun was shining, and Amanda was glad about that. There were only a few days until December arrived, and that meant a higher risk for snow. The trip was long, but they talked the entire way, finally arriving in Alton, Illinois, several hours later. Jim decided to check in at the bed and breakfast first before going to the river.

It was a beautiful gray-colored Victorian home with white trim on the windows and white lace-like spindles bordering the front porch. A porch swing and white rocking chairs stood invitingly on each side of the dark wooden door. Inside on the main level, there were several burgundy floral printed rugs spread on top of a distressed wood floor. An elaborate hand-carved staircase led to the second-floor rooms. The wallpaper was a cream-colored floral print with splashes of burgundy and green throughout the pattern.

After admiring the décor and relishing a bygone era, they walked toward the check-in counter where a smiling elderly woman stood.

"Good afternoon," she said as they approached the counter.

"Hello," Jim responded. "There should be a reservation here for *Dorion*."

The woman nodded. "Yes, I took your reservation myself. Welcome to Alton, Mr. Dorion." She handed him a couple of keys. "Enjoy your stay. My name's

Elizabeth, and please feel free to call the desk if you need anything. This house has been in my family for generations, and it's a pleasure to have guests."

"Thanks," Jim said. "We're happy to be here as well."

"Your home is absolutely stunning," Amanda said.

"Indeed, it is," Karen added. "I can't wait to see more of it."

Elizabeth seemed pleased with the compliments. She smiled broadly and said, "Thank you. One more thing. I'll be serving dinner with wine at six o'clock if you plan on eating here this evening. You're the only guests here tonight, so just let me know if you're coming. I won't cook anything if you'd rather eat in town."

Jim looked at Karen and Amanda. They nodded to indicate they wanted to eat at the bed and breakfast. "We'll stay here," he confirmed.

Elizabeth again seemed pleased. "That's great. It sounds crazy, but I like to cook for people. I'll make breakfast for you in the morning, too. There is no extra charge to your bill."

They carried their bags upstairs. Karen and Amanda's key had the number *10* engraved on it, and the room was located across the hall from Jim's. There was a full bathroom at the end of the hall. Amanda was glad there weren't any other guests staying the night. She wasn't a fan of sharing a bathroom with strangers. The walls in the room were painted blue with a floral wallpaper border near the ceiling, and there were two ornately carved wooden beds covered with patchwork quilts. Amanda suspected that Elizabeth had made the quilts herself. Karen was standing quietly at the window, so she joined her. Together, they admired the pretty gazebo that stood in the middle of the backyard.

There was a knock on the door, and then Jim said, "It's me."

Amanda opened the door and smiled. "Hello, *me.*"

"Ha, Ha. We should probably go to the river now," he said, grinning.

They decided to walk to get there. Amanda had never seen the Mississippi River, and she was surprised at how calm it appeared. She knew, though, that looks can be deceiving when it came to water.

As they stood on the muddy bank, Jim pulled a gray stone from his messenger bag and showed it to Amanda. The chiseled words said, *In honor of Margarethe Mueller, with love from her family.*

"It's beautiful," she said.

Jim then turned to Karen. "I think you should toss it in there."

"I'd be honored," Karen said. She took the stone from his hand and traced Margarethe's name with her finger, as if committing it to memory. And then, she tossed it. Gentle ripples encircled the stone as it sunk into the dark water.

They stood quietly and waited until the ripples ceased, and then Jim said, "You know, it's rather bittersweet that Margarethe survived that beating, only to be killed by another man at a later time."

"Yes, it is," Karen agreed. "But if it weren't for her survival, we wouldn't be here. Knowing her story has changed my attitude on life. It's given me strength because if an immigrant woman can live through what she did—the brutal attack, having to testify against the man in an American court, requesting a divorce during a time when this would have been scorned, enduring the persecution by her community, and then having the strength to marry again and have children—I should be able to stand strong."

"Knowing about Margarethe changed my outlook on life, as well," Jim agreed. "In a sense, I believe we owe it to her to do something meaningful—to ensure that her struggle was not in vain."

"That's a great way to look at it," Amanda said.

Jim cleared his throat and looked into her eyes. "Karen and I have talked about a lot of things during the past few days. One topic that came up several times was about how we could help abused women. We inherited a large sum of money when our parents died, and Margarethe's story has made us realize we should put some of it to good use. We'd like to open a shelter for women and their children to escape from abuse. It will be called the Margarethe Mueller Recovery Institute, and we'd like for you to be the director of recovery."

Amanda was stunned, and it took her a second to be able to speak. "I don't know what to say. I'm honored, but I need to think about it," she stammered.

"Just say, *yes!*" Karen said. "I'll be working there, too. I never told you, but I'm an accountant, and I'll be handling the books."

"I understand you'd like to think about it," Jim said, "but I hope you'll do it."

"Where will it be located?" Amanda asked.

"We've found a large house with 20 acres near Paola, but we're not making an offer until you see it. The acreage will provide enough space to build a larger facility in the future. There will also be room for each family's pets if they bring them, and we'll have farm animals, too. A large garden and walking trail will be added later. Of course, we'll need to add security measures to protect the women from harm, in case an abuser finds the place."

"Hmm," Amanda said. "It does sound wonderful. Let me sleep on it. I'm beginning to think that my calling might be in solving family history mysteries, and then helping people to heal from any trauma incurred from previous generations."

Jim smiled. "You could do that at the Institute if you'd like, or you can do it on the side."

Amanda was excited, but she still wanted to think about it before giving an answer. They walked back to the bed and breakfast for dinner, but they needed to clean their muddy shoes before going inside. They decided to leave them on the porch to dry, so they wouldn't leave footprints on the rugs and wood floors. Elizabeth must have been watching for them because she opened the door to let them inside. She handed them each a pair of stretchable sock slippers.

"Your feet will be cold if you don't put these on," she said.

"Thank you so much," Amanda said.

"That's very kind of you," Karen added.

Jim was skeptical. "Not sure if they will fit my big feet, but I'll try." He soon found, though, that they fit just fine.

The house was warm and smelled of a good hot meal. Elizabeth ushered them into the dining room, where the table had been set up with a bottle of wine, glasses, ceramic plates, and silverware.

"This is wonderful," Jim said. "You've gone to a lot of trouble, and it is much appreciated."

Elizabeth's face flushed. "No trouble at all. I told you I like to cook. Please have a seat and drink a glass of wine if you'd like. I'll bring in dinner momentarily."

Amanda, Karen, and Jim sat down and poured themselves a glass of wine.

"What a lovely place and a nice lady," Amanda said. "How did you find it?"

"I just looked up places to stay on the internet and it popped up. The reviews were all good, so I made a reservation."

"Dinner certainly smells good," Karen said, taking a sip of wine.

Elizabeth hurried into the dining room carrying a large plate of pot roast, carrots, and potatoes. "Enjoy," she said, placing it on the table.

"That looks delicious," Amanda said. "Thank you."

"It certainly does," Jim agreed.

Karen was first to fill her plate. "I can't wait to try it," she said.

After Amanda and Jim filled up their plates, they each took their first bite and declared that it was the best pot roast they'd ever tasted. Elizabeth stood near the table and beamed. "Thanks. It was my late husband's favorite meal," she said.

"Well, he certainly had good taste in food and in women, too," Amanda said. "You've been so kind to us. I feel like I'm at home here."

"That means a lot to me."

"Would you like to sit down and eat with us?" Jim asked.

"I've already eaten, but I appreciate the invitation. You all go right ahead and enjoy yourselves. I'll come back later to clear everything away. Don't you do a thing except have a nice evening together."

"Okay," Karen said, smiling. "I think we can do that, especially with this terrific meal."

"Thank you and goodnight," Elizabeth said, turning to go back to the kitchen.

Their dinner was filled with high-spirited laughter, and then Karen excused herself early so she could take a shower and go to bed—which left Amanda and Jim at the table. They sipped their wine and talked more about the Margarethe Mueller Recovery Institute. Jim was very persuasive.

"Okay," Amanda said, "I'm in. You've convinced me, and I'm thrilled."

"Well, that's great!"

Jim suggested they go outside for a walk to see the old stately houses around the town. Their shoes were dry, so they removed their sock slippers and put them back on before venturing on their tour. The streetlights guided them through the dark along the tree-lined sidewalk. Amanda looked at each home, wondering about the history of each—the people who lived there and what their dreams might have been. At the end of the block, Jim stopped and turned to face her, and she knew what would come next. He leaned toward her, and she, toward him, before the long-awaited kiss. It was unfortunate that Jim's arm was in a sling, because Amanda wanted to embrace him tightly. But the kiss was wonderful—actually, the best she'd ever had. Afterward, Jim said, "I've been wanting to do that for a long time. You're the most amazing person I've ever met."

Amanda looked into his eyes and smiled, "And I feel the same about you."

They held hands and walked back to the bed and breakfast, and then shared one last goodnight kiss before going to their separate rooms.

Amanda was too ecstatic to sleep that night, so no dreams came to her. Not that it mattered. She was now living the best kind of dream. Early the next morning, she and Karen packed up and met Jim downstairs for breakfast.

Elizabeth did not disappoint. Once again, she had laid out a nice table—this time with a basket of warm blueberry muffins and a large plate of mixed fruit. As soon as they were seated, she entered the dining room carrying a metal carafe of coffee and placed it on the table.

"I hope this is enough for you to eat before your trip back home," she said.

"It's perfect," Amanda responded.

"Everything has been wonderful. We'll come here again," Jim added.

Karen nodded. "Hopefully, sooner than later."

"I hope so, too," Elizabeth said, turning to leave.

"I'll come pay the bill when we're done eating," Jim called.

"No problem. Take your time."

And they did. They drank coffee and ate muffins for nearly an hour before deciding to leave. Jim paid the bill, and then they each had several bathroom breaks before they loaded their bags and left.

"I guess we shouldn't have had so much coffee," Amanda said, laughing.

"Indeed," Jim said. "But it was fun, and that makes it worthwhile."

"I certainly enjoyed our time together here, even though we came for a rather sad reason," Karen said as she started the car and pulled away.

"I know what you mean," Jim agreed. "We can't change history though. All we can do is acknowledge it and remember those who came before us. We're doing that. Although Margarethe lived long ago—her life mattered. Her strong spirit helped her endure an unthinkable trauma, and that strong spirit still remains within us."

Karen nodded with tears in her eyes. "Well said, Jim."

Amanda decided to give her opinion. "I believe that even though the effects of trauma might be passed down as anxiety or depression through the generations, perhaps resilience and strength can also develop. Maybe just knowing what happened to Margarethe and how she managed to live her life after the beating has brought about some healing. That's just my opinion. There's no proof of this."

"I believe that," Karen agreed. "I haven't had a nightmare about it for a long time, and I feel stronger now."

"That is wonderful," Amanda said.

The rest of the ride home was filled with enthusiastic banter, as if tossing the stone into the river had released Jim and Karen from the heavy burden of the past.

Carolyn's car was parked in Amanda's driveway when they arrived.

"Looks like you have company," Karen said as she parked.

"I hope it's someone you know," Jim said hesitantly.

"That's my friend's car," Amanda said. "You should both come in to meet her." She picked up her overnight bag and motioned for them to follow.

Carolyn met them at the door with an excited dog at her side. "Welcome home," she said as she opened the door wider to let them inside. "I just stopped by to feed your doggie." She eyed Jim and Karen curiously.

Amanda set her bag on the floor and squatted down to pet Bandy. "Thanks so much for taking care of her," she said, standing up again. "I'd like to introduce you to Jim and Karen Dorion."

Carolyn smiled and extended her hand first to Jim and then to Karen. "It's a pleasure to meet you."

"Likewise," Jim responded, grinning.

"It's nice to meet you, too," Karen said.

Carolyn smiled at Amanda. "I hope you had a nice trip. Everything has been fine here."

"It was great," she said.

There was an awkward pause until Carolyn spoke again. "Well, I should be going. I need to go check on my kids."

"Okay. Thanks again," Amanda said, reaching out to hug her.

Carolyn smiled after they embraced, and then winked as she turned to leave. "Nice to meet you," she called as she walked out the door.

As if on cue, Karen announced she would wait in the car for Jim, and she walked out as well. This left Jim and Amanda alone. They still couldn't embrace due to the sling on his arm, so they leaned toward each other for another kiss.

"It's hard to leave," Jim said, stroking Amanda's cheek.

"I have a feeling we'll be seeing each other a lot though."

"Indeed, we will. I'll call you tomorrow, so we can set up a time for you to see the house in Paola."

Amanda snickered. "I'll have to look at my calendar."

"You do that, and then pencil me in on your busy schedule."

And with that, Jim walked back to the car with a grin on his face.

Chapter 19

In the upcoming weeks, Amanda would agree with Jim and Karen that the land and home in Paola would be the perfect place for the Margarethe Mueller Recovery Institute. After the holidays, they hired a contractor to handle the renovations to the house. If all went as planned, the Institute would open in June. Amanda's role would indeed include helping certain clients solve mysteries of their past if there was an indication of trauma in the family background. She was a strong researcher and had the love of a good mystery, so she was quite excited about what the future might hold—especially when it came to Jim. They were falling rapidly in love with each other, and she suspected their future would be made together.

Jim's bullet wound healed nicely, so he was able to begin physical therapy to restore muscle tone. Of course, there was a scar which would never be fully erased, but it would serve as a reminder of survival.

Hank decided to continue volunteering at the cemetery. On a sunny day in March, he called Jim to say that Sophia's headstone had arrived, so they all went to see it. Her chiseled name appeared to be in the same font style as what was used on Margarethe's stone—a small final link between a mother and daughter who had endured so much. As Jim, Karen, and Amanda stood near Sophia's headstone, a chilly breeze began to blow. They stood in quiet respect for a woman they didn't know.

They walked back to the cemetery office to say goodbye to Hank, who had remained there to give them some privacy. He'd made a pot of coffee for them, so they sat down and talked for another hour. They would have stayed longer, but Debbie called to invite him to have dinner with her. He grinned as he clicked off the phone.

"Looks like I have a date," he said.

"We'll let you get to that, then," Jim said, standing up and stretching. "Where would you like for us to put our cups?"

"Just leave them," Hank answered. "I'll pick them up later."

Jim shook his hand. "Good to see you again."

"You, too. We should meet for dinner soon."

Jim nodded. "Let's plan on going out to celebrate when the Institute opens."

"That would be great."

Amanda and Karen took turns giving Hank a hug, and then he said, "I never thought I'd find such good friends by volunteering in a cemetery office. And, of course, I never thought it would be dangerous here either, but it all turned out okay. Here we are months later, and I couldn't be happier." He then walked them out the door and stood there and waved as they pulled away in Jim's Subaru.

The month of March passed quickly, and April's arrival ushered in spring's first days of warmer weather. Amanda celebrated her favorite season by once again enjoying time on her deck and watching Bandy chase squirrels. However, she was no longer alone each day as she had been months before. Jim sat at her side quite often, and they watched as the landscape changed from the drab brown of winter to a marvelous shade of green. The trees were budding, and the flowers were beginning to bloom, and

Amanda felt the same sense of renewal in her own life. Gone were the days when she'd felt burned out in her job—when running back home was her only way to escape. Fleeing, as it turned out, was not an escape at all. Amanda had unknowingly run toward something instead—a life of making new memories with friends and a very special man. The dream of the two lovers on horses had not appeared to her for months, and she knew that it would probably never come again. As she'd realized months before, she'd found the person of her dreams. And although he didn't ride in on a horse, Jim came into her life with the same allure of a fairy tale. She now looked forward to helping others at the Institute.

Never wanting to leave any loose ends, Amanda finished the painting of the farm scene she'd started, which had been sitting on the easel in her office for several months. In fact, she had begun a new one, which was a more contemporary piece with vibrant colors. Jim liked both paintings so much that he asked if she'd be willing to hang them at the Institute. She was thrilled at the prospect of hanging her art, but Jim's request also gave her an idea. She decided that since art can bring healing and comfort to the soul, she wanted to conduct painting classes at the Institute. Jim and Karen thought it was a great idea, so they agreed to designate a special space for that to happen. And in that special space, Jim had one thing he wanted to add. He presented it to Amanda one morning as they sat down to drink coffee on her deck. It was a large photograph of an English bulldog riding a skateboard with a calico cat on its back. She laughed and clapped her hand over her mouth. "Where on earth did you get this?"

Jim merely winked and said, "I have connections. It will add a bit of fun to your art classroom, don't you think?"

Amanda, still laughing, said, "Indeed, it will. Thank you!"

Karen's nightmares had disappeared completely, and she was now reclaiming her own life with a renewed spirit. It was unfortunate, however, that even though they continued to search, there were still no clues as to what had happened to Hans Mueller. Senator Bart Kleiner had stopped talking. And although Jim and Karen didn't like to mention the upcoming trial, Amanda knew they would be called to testify. However, she was confident they would handle it bravely and justice would be served, and perhaps the truth about what became of Hans would be revealed at that time. She had a feeling that it would, and her intuition had always served her well. After all, she had a strong feeling to return Jim's call months before, and things had turned out remarkably well. In fact, life was better than she had ever expected it would be, and for that, Amanda was extremely thankful.

ABOUT THE AUTHOR

 R. J. Rein is a graduate from the William Allen White School of Journalism at the University of Kansas. A former greeting card writer and advertising copywriter, she's now sharpened her quill for mysteries. She lives in Overland Park, Kansas with her husband and son.

Author's Note

Memories of Malice is a work of fiction, but my second great-grandmother was beaten after she immigrated to the United States in the late 1800s.

As I wrote this book, I came upon information about ancestral trauma and epigenetics. Scientific studies have indicated the possibility that the effects of trauma experienced by an ancestor could be passed down for generations. Although these studies have been somewhat controversial, they made me reflect on how an ancestor's life could impact their descendants.

The town of Osawatomie, Kansas, is real, and the state mental institution is located there. The address of 755 Whispering Meadow Lane does not exist, nor does a woman named Amanda Latham live at such an address.

The towns of Hillsdale and Paola are also real, and they are a short distance from Osawatomie. There is a cemetery in Hillsdale, but no one by the name of Hank Autin volunteers there, nor was such a man ever admitted to the hospital in Paola.

Overland Park, Kansas is a suburb of Kansas City, but there is no one named Jim Dorion living there with a sister named Karen—at least not that I'm aware of.

Alton, Illinois, is home to some lovely bed and breakfast inns, but the one created for this story does not exist.

There's also no senator like the man described in this book, nor have I ever heard of one who resembles his character.

www.ingramcontent.com/pod-product-compliance
Lightning Source LLC
Chambersburg PA
CBHW020325260626
47156CB00004B/1376